IMMORTAL

The House of Ganymede

Robert A. Karl

Published by Robert A. Karl

First Edition May 2025

ISBN: 979-8-9929513-0-1 (paperback)

ISBN: 979-8-9929513-1-8 (ebook)

This book is entirely the author's creation. AI was not used in any way, and the use of the contents of this book for AI machine learning is expressly forbidden.

Cover Design: Krishna (fiverr.com/nirkri)

Images licensed through Shutterstock.

"Ganymede, who was the loveliest
born of the race of mortals,
and therefore the gods caught him away to themselves,
to be Zeus's wine-pourer."
Homer, The Iliad, Greek epic, 8th Century BCE

Contents

Introduction

I MMORTAL: The House of Ganymede
A Queer novel for Young Adults

IMMORTAL: The House of Ganymede is inspired by the story of the mortal shepherd from Troy, as told in Greek mythology. Zeus, the king of the gods and the ruler of Mount Olympus, took the form of an eagle and abducted Ganymede due to his exceptional beauty, having him serve as the cup-bearer to the gods and granting him immortality.

In this modern re-interpretation, Jason, an exceptionally handsome young man, is pursued by the Greek billionaire owner of ZEUS Universal Group, a world leader in the development of artificial intelligence and robotics, who is visiting the site of their new data center, which will use hydroelectric power from nearby Niagara Falls. Will Jason, who is just beginning to explore his Queer identity, be lured by the promise of a life of luxury and fame? Can he remain true to himself if he agrees to become the face of IMMORTAL, a new line of self-care products for men? What sacrifices must he make? And, in the midst of change, can he find his true love?

This story, for young adults, is about identity, independence, loyalty, friendship, romance, and the price one must pay in the pursuit of success.

CW: Violence
Suicide

Chapter One

G rinning, Jason strolled into the first day of his English 3 class with his confidence level set at ultra-high. His reputation as a quiet kid in school, well-earned in his freshman and sophomore years, was about to end.

Taking his seat, he glanced at his bestie Timmy, about to become his co-conspirator in disrupting the class. He winked, and Jason nodded back in agreement. Today was the day they'd been waiting for, and the moment for them to seize attention was getting close.

Trying to stifle a sneeze, Jason silently wished that the school could somehow ban the use of cheap perfumes and colognes. It seemed that no one in this small town, or at least no one in the Junior class at Niagara County High School, had any sense of style.

As the other students settled into their seats, Jason lifted his head in Timmy's direction, shifting his bright blue eyes to the student sitting two seats away. Following Jason's gaze, Timmy suddenly noticed the new student, surely destined to become one of the most sought-after girls in school. The look on his face when he turned back to Jason was priceless.

Placing his hand to cover his face from the view of most of the class, he made a licking motion with his tongue between two raised fingers, rolled his eyes, and then broke out into laughter.

"Down boy!" Jason whispered. "We'll get our chance with that luscious peach soon enough. Let's remember our mission here."

"Sir, yes, sir!" he replied, mimicking the JROTC (Junior Reserve Officers' Training Corps) students at the school, a frequent target of their ridicule. Unlike those students, neither Jason nor Timmy had any interest in a military career.

Ignoring him, Jason's attention turned once more to the freshly blooming flower of girlhood just out of his reach. That's something he hoped would change soon, as he watched the sunlight playfully jumping through her long, dark, straight hair, imagining his fingers darting through the strands.

"Welcome Juuuuuuniors!" Mr. Simmons called out in his booming, theatrical voice. "I've been looking forward all summer to finally getting to meet all of you. Rumor has it that there are more than a few characters in this class."

He smiled as his eyes met each student's gaze, making everyone feel as though he really cared about them, not just as a class, but as individual people.

That's one reason Mr. Simmons became one of the most popular teachers in the school. Being relatively young at around the age of 30 and definitely handsome also helped his cause.

"Being admitted into my Honors English class is both an honor and a privilege. I want to be clear that I have very high expectations for each and every one of you. And, just in case you didn't check your roster carefully, I want you to understand that this class only meets twice a week, but for a double period every Tuesday and Thursday. Keep that in mind when working on your assignments. Late submissions are not tolerated here, so don't even try it."

"What if my mom has cancer and I have to visit her in the hospital?" Debi called out angrily.

The air was heavy with sighs from the students who knew Debi all too well. Her constant complaints and "what ifs" about everything and anything were beyond annoying.

Mr. Simmons, however, displayed no sign of irritation or annoyance.

"Of course," he replied, "valid reasons will be taken seriously and will be taken into consideration. However, Ms. Hampton, I had the opportunity to chat with your mother at the faculty and school board luncheon last week, and she seemed perfectly healthy to me. And she never mentioned that she was ill. Please have her reach out to me if she wants your work to be accepted late for any reason whatsoever."

The classroom erupted in laughter as the teacher put Debi in her place. Ignoring the reaction of her classmates, Debi insisted on having the last word.

"You better believe she'll be contacting the administration about the disrespectful attitude of the faculty here," she retorted, sitting back and folding her arms in a show of disdain for the teacher's authority.

Jason tended to ignore spats between teachers and students. He wasn't interested in power struggles, at least, not any involving true authority figures. His hands were full enough with the badgering he endured from his classmates during the last two years.

Never from the girls in his class. They adored him, even if they knew nothing about him. Why? His incredible beauty.

Sometimes, the girls would argue whether Jason was handsome or if he would be better described as pretty. Or beautiful. Or gorgeous. Or sexy.

Jason, however, was unamused by such talk. He accepted his looks as a fact of life, never really thinking about the implications.

It was more difficult for him to ignore the taunts from the boys in his class. "Baby Face." "Pretty Boy." Even "Girly Boy."

He wanted to be accepted as one of the guys, without being labeled in a way that made him feel weak or effeminate. That's why he had this plan to re-introduce himself as someone strong, manly, and not at all feminine.

His thoughts were interrupted when Mr. Simmons began to give the instructions for the assignment. No one was surprised to hear him say, "Prepare a short introduction about yourself. Make it like an Instagram reel, but avoid making a video with you just talking about yourself. Incorporate various media, including videos, photos, sounds, GIFs, and other images — whatever you like. And don't tell us your entire life story. Keep it current. For example, you might focus on what you did this past summer."

This was exactly what Jason and Timmy had planned for. A presentation about "What I Did During Summer Vacation." Predictable for a first-day assignment, but not unwelcome.

"Spend an hour working, and then we'll watch and comment on the presentations during the second hour. If you need to record anything, find a quiet spot outside of the classroom for that. We'll meet back here in one hour. Now, take those laptops and start creating!"

Jason's assignment was already completed, well before the first day of school. He downloaded it from the cloud, easily bypassing the school's feeble attempt at web security. With nothing to do, he went outside to relax, finding a comfortable spot to sit under a massive old oak tree, that had already started dropping its acorns. Fall comes early to this part of

New York State, with Niagara Falls just a few miles up the road.

Relaxing against the sturdy oak, he watched as an eagle soared through the cloudless sky, most probably in search of prey. As the regal bird swooped down and out of sight, Timmy sat beside his friend, since his presentation was also completed before class even began.

"Look, I think it's a bald eagle," he said quietly to Jason, as if he were worried that his voice would frighten the bird. "And he has a fish."

"I wonder if the fish is scared or has any idea what's about to happen to it," Timmy continued.

"Ohh, I hope not," Jason replied. "It's already struggling to breathe and feeling pain from those talons. Imagine if it just survived going over the Falls, only to end up as lunch for that eagle. What a fate, right?"

As the eagle flew off into the distance, out of sight, Jason wondered what it must be like to rule the skies with impunity. He envied the eagle, which had the freedom to soar wherever it wanted to go, through the air, not having to consider hiking paths or roads.

"Eagles are magnificent creatures, that's for sure," was all he said, as more students were coming outside, with a few joining in at the base of the tree.

Teenage boys will most likely identify with animals such as the eagle — embodying strength, agility, and freedom. They don't see themselves as the fish, caught in the talons, desperate to escape. Their failure to recognize the claws holding them tightly, forcing them into situations where conformity and uniformity are the norm, leaves them powerless to resist. You cannot escape your bonds if you don't even realize that you are being held in bondage.

The blush showing on Timmy's face as a gaggle of giggling girls joins them under the oak tree is a sure sign of his interest. He's determined to get a girlfriend this year, and part of his plan is included in his presentation for English class today. He has high hopes that what he says will spark some interest.

"I like the way you're letting your hair grow longer," Bella said to Jason, whose blonde locks are just over his ears, the thick, wavy strands moving slightly in the gentle afternoon breeze. "That buzz cut you had all last year was cute — for a sophomore," she kidded.

Jason smiled wanly at her, not overly interested in her comments. He considered Bella to be rather plain-looking, though all the other boys in class would describe her as pretty.

"Who're you taking to the prom?" Susan Malone asked, looking at Timmy. She had been interested in him since the 6th Grade, but had no luck in getting him to ask her on a date. She let out a yawn and stretched, raising her arms above her head, shaking her breasts, which had grown considerably larger over the summer break. That got Timmy's attention, though he made a decent attempt not to stare.

"Prom? It's too soon to think about the prom. And that's a serious decision I'll be making much later on," he intoned, trying to lower his voice and sound serious. "However, there are plenty of dances and other activities before the prom, so maybe we can ..."

"I'd love to!" Susan cut in. "Just let me know where and when, and ... and ..."

Suddenly, Susan remembered how to play the game. She knew better than to appear that anxious to go on a date with Timmy. "And I'll check my schedule and let you know."

The other girls signaled that Susan had saved herself from embarrassment. Everyone has to be careful to follow the social norms when trying to navigate the perils of high school in the 21st Century.

As the group chatted about their plans for the upcoming school year, Jason was aware of the group of guys who had assembled close-by. Ignoring those around him, he focused on the comments being made by the other group.

"He is pretty, isn't he? And check out that hair of his. Growing it out like that, he'll probably be trying out for the role of Goldilocks in the school play," one boy snickered.

"Yeah, us guys can be the three bears, right? Eat some of that bitch's porridge and put him in his place," another exclaimed.

"If not Goldilocks, maybe he'll be Rapunzel. I'll volunteer to climb up his hair and then show him how a man treats his woman!"

Evil laughter rose from the group of teen boys, making fun of a classmate based on his appearance and fantasizing about how they might abuse him.

Jason wanted nothing more than to be accepted by his peers. Male and female. He wanted to find a way to get the boys in his class to see him in a different light. Not as an object to be ridiculed.

He doesn't even understand why they treat him this way. True, he is beautiful, but doesn't that mean that one should also be popular? Is it jealousy? Or does some other factor drive their disapproval?

Jason is determined to find the answers to these questions and a solution to the problem that he's facing.

Timmy is the only boy in the class who accepts Jason completely. Best friends since the first grade, Timmy is unaware of the distance between Jason and the other boys in the class. He just never notices things like that, since his mind is mostly focused on the girls in the class and how to get to know them better.

Just before the group heads back to class, Timmy says, "Hey Jase, how about a fishing trip this weekend? Maybe we can hit Devil's Hole and catch some rainbows. My mom will let us have a fish fry if we have a good catch, and maybe we can invite a couple of honeys to join us."

Timmy's smile at Susan when he mentions the "honeys" causes her heart to flutter with anticipation. *Maybe this weekend, it'll finally happen!* she thinks.

Jason waits for his friends to walk back toward the classroom, watching them a few steps ahead as he finally begins to follow them. His attention is focused on Timmy, his best friend for years. But now, something seems different. Jason, ignoring the female forms before him, only has eyes for Timmy, who is maturing into an athletic male.

Jason admires his powerful strides as Timmy walks along, still trying to impress the girls. He has to admit to himself that Timmy has been in his thoughts almost constantly, especially at night, just before he goes to sleep. And he knows the word that best describes his thoughts of Timmy.

That he's sexy. Yes, sexy. Jason's breath comes just a bit faster as he contemplates that thought.

As he enters the building, Jason hears the cry of another eagle circling the skies, searching for prey. At the same moment, he feels the eyes of his predators, the group of boys in his class, following closely behind him.

His confidence begins to falter. Why is life so difficult? Why can't people just be nice to one another? Why is everything such a struggle? His shoulders droop as he enters the classroom for the presentations.

"Yes, Debi, you can be the first to present," Mr. Simmons tells the daughter of the School Board President. As she begins, Jason zones out, with no interest in whatever boring teenage nonsense Debi had engaged in during the past summer. Instead, his eyes were closed, as he was engaged in daydreaming about his weekend plans with Timmy. Going to the lake, fishing, and maybe ... well, maybe that would be the day that Jason would tell him what he'd been thinking about recently.

And Timmy had mentioned catching rainbows. Sure, he may have meant catching some trout, since rainbows are a common variety found in the waters here, but maybe he meant something else. A hidden message. A secret meaning. Jason's imagination ran wild, as he thought of him and Timmy stripping down to their undies, maybe even less, running and jumping like water sprites, chasing and occasionally catching rainbows, their lithe bodies glistening in the bright sunlight.

Was it possible that this coming weekend might be the day when their lips would first touch lightly, and Jason would finally experience the taste that he so desperately longed for?

"Mr. Masters. Mr. Masters. Earth calling Jason Masters!"

Jason suddenly became aware that the teacher was calling his name, expecting him to share his presentation. It took a moment for Jason to recover and return to his present circumstances, sitting in English class at Niagara County High School.

He remembered that his main goal for today was to amuse his classmates, hoping that they'd see him in a different light this year. He hoped they'd be impressed with what he was about to show them.

His presentation began with a blank screen for about three seconds, and then the title, written with dark red letters, dripping in blood:

My Killercation at Niagara Falls

Jason was pleased to see the rapt attention from both his classmates and their teacher, as the song, "I Know What You Did Last Summer" by Shawn Mendes and Camila Cabello began to play, followed by scenes from their music video for the song. However, Jason had replaced the Shawn Mendes character with himself, in what he considered a genius move. Interspersed with scenes from the video, he showed the poster for the movie of the same name, with his face added to those already pictured: Sarah Michelle Gellar, Freddie Prinze Jr., Jennifer Love Hewitt, and Ryan Phillippe. As the soundtrack continued, he included elements from the movie, inserting himself into key scenes, so it looked like he was involved in the story about the teens being stalked by a hook-wielding killer.

At the very end of the presentation, he placed himself in the role of the killer, laughing menacingly at the camera and saying, "And that's how I spent my summer killercation!"

Jason held his breath, waiting for a response from the class. Kyle, one of the boys who usually expressed disdain for Jason, said, "Damn, that was actually decent, man!" bringing a smile to Jason's face.

"Creative, entertaining, and definitely an attention-getter," commented the teacher. "However, not very informative, unless you actually spent the summer on a murder spree."

"Really? You're gonna drag me for not telling you more about my boring summer activities?" Jason shot back.

"The teacher's right. You didn't really do the assignment properly," added Debi, always one to follow rules strictly.

"Don't be such a downer," Susan chimed in. "It was excellent. And much better than that boring story you told about eating hot dogs at the Falls. Like a hot dog is all you had in your mouth this summer," Susan snidely added, eliciting laughter from the class.

Debi couldn't help showing her fury at the nasty comment, being fiercely guarded about her reputation.

"All right. Let's cool it down," Mr. Simmons warned. "It was a good presentation, though off-topic. Enough said about that. Let's continue."

Timmy was next, and since he already had a reputation as a class clown, no one knew what to expect, especially since his best friend, Jason, had just surprised everyone with his project.

Timmy was determined not to disappoint, and he hoped to even out-do his bestie, so he leaned forward with anticipation as his presentation began.

The title: I Don't Want To Be A 40-Year-Old Virgin

The class erupted in laughter and applause.

The presentation was a series of slides, showing almost every girl in the school, with Timmy inserted into each photo, acting as if he were begging each girl to be with him. Captions included:

"Please, please, please let me be close to you. Like, really, really, really close!" as he knelt in front of one of the class beauties.

"I got needs, babe. I can't wait forever, you know," with a photo of him leering at a different female classmate.

"I told all the guys I lost my virginity in the 8th Grade, but I lied!" as he was shown standing alone, winking at the camera.

At the end of the show, he added a video of him dancing solo to "Like A Virgin" by Madonna.

The closing shot was Timmy saying, "I spent my summer vacation trying my best to lose my virginity," as he shrugged his shoulders, turned, and walked off-camera.

The class never stopped laughing, and there was a solid round of applause as the screen faded to black.

Timmy was well aware that the subject of a guy's virginity status was a sensitive subject, especially in the Junior year of high school. He also knew that most guys would assume he'd never approach the subject unless he had already had one or more sexual encounters. His expectations were met as all the guys in the class were applauding and nodding approvingly.

Now, he figured no one would ever accuse him of being a virgin again.

Even the teacher commented, "Well, that was brave of you, Mr. Connor. And may I congratulate you on your accomplishment this summer," he said, smiling broadly.

Jason's thoughts returned to daydreams of Timmy while other students told their stories. He didn't really care if Timmy had been with a girl or not. His thoughts turned to whether Timmy had ever thought of him in a different way.

It would be awesome if Timmy would make the first move, he thought.

Jason once more paid attention as the new girl in class was the next to present. She introduced herself as Youngmi Kwon, explaining that her name, when translated from Korean to English, would mean "Forever Powerful."

"Wow!" Jason whispered under his breath. *She's gorgeous, and if that name describes her, she's just my type,* he thought, forgetting for just a minute about his growing feelings for Timmy.

Her presentation focused on her family moving from Korea to the United States, with her father taking a position as an executive at ZEUS Universal Group.

Oh my god, she's probably rich, too, Jason continued thinking.

Once she finished, she turned to say to the class, "I hope to find new friends here. I'm excited to be here in America."

That's when her eyes met Jason's, and both of them felt an instant connection. They both smiled, getting lost in the moment, only seeing each other, as if the rest of the class had vanished.

However, the rest of the class was busy observing the obvious attraction between the two.

"Looks like someone's gonna be eating Chinese tonight!" one boy called out. Every boy in the class, and a few of the girls, were laughing, but then quickly turned silent, seeing the look of anger on Jason's face.

"Who said that?" demanded Jason. "Who's the rude boy?"

Total silence from the class, including the teacher.

"You! What's your name?" demanded Youngmi, pointing at a skinny, pimply-faced boy with greasy brown hair.

"Me? Why me?" the boy said, trying to feign his innocence. But Youngmi had seen the culprit and had no fear in calling him out.

"Your name, now!" she demanded.

"I'm Bannon. Charles Bannon. And it was just a little joke. Chill, girlie."

At that, Jason jumped from his chair, ready to pounce.

"No need to defend me, Killer," Youngmi said, winking at Jason. "I can handle myself, especially with little bitch boys like Charlie over there."

She turned her attention once more to Bannon.

"I heard about you already, and it's only the first half of my first day here," she said, standing and moving toward Bannon, shaking her finger in his direction.

"Yes, Charles Bannon. That's the name I heard some of the girls talking about during first period this morning. I definitely remember they said you were the President of the SPS here at school. Is that true?"

"Girls were talking about me?" he said, seemingly confused. Charles was among the least popular of all the boys, and he never imagined anyone, especially a group of girls, giving him a second thought.

"Is it true?" Youngmi demanded again.

"I don't know. I think so. I'm the President of what again?"

"SPS. Yes or no?"

"Yes, that's me," Charles replied, not sensing the trap.

"Ha! There you have it, ladies. Just like you said. Charles Bannon has declared that he is the President of the Small Penis Society here at Niagara County High!"

The laughter from the class at Bannon's plight could be heard all the way to the Principal's office.

"All right. All right. That's enough," came the stern warning from Mr. Simmons, quickly regaining control of the situation.

"Mr. Bannon, step up front. Now."

Charles, trying to overcome his humiliation, approached the teacher's desk.

"Well?" Mr. Simmons demanded.

"I'm sorry. I was wrong. I didn't really mean any offense."

Youngmi said, "I didn't come here looking to make any enemies, especially not on the first day. I'm sorry, too," she said. Turning back to Jason, she said, "Thanks for having my back, Killer. And your presentation was wicked. I loved it!"

Jason beamed at the compliment, his smile making him even more beautiful. He was already thinking ahead to the prom and possibly taking the gorgeous new girl as his date.

While other students showed their work, Jason composed an email to Mr. Simmons.

"Here's my alternate presentation, in case you care more about content than style," he wrote, attaching a file with a story about his boring summer filled with mundane activities.

"P.S. I did all the readings on the summer reading list. I'm looking forward to learning a lot from you about literature, especially about the themes of these works."

Jason paused before sending the message. Mr. Simmons was about to show his presentation, sharing what he had done during summer vacation.

All eyes were on the screen at the front of the class, as the first image appeared. A sign, saying, "Fire Island National Seashore," dissolved into a still photo of Mr. Simmons standing next to the sign, dissolving again into a photo of Mr. Simmons and another, unknown young man, standing arm-in-arm while leaning against the sign.

You could already hear the whispers beginning from a few of the students, speculating about their English teacher.

Jason glanced quickly in Mr. Simmons's direction, for the first time realizing just how handsome he was, and now he began to wonder about his assumptions.

Then, a montage of quick cuts, showing the teacher and his companion sunning themselves on the beach, eating at several of the restaurants at the famous vacation spot, at night clubs surrounded by groups of men, the two of them dancing together, and ending with a quick glimpse of them kissing.

Kissing!

A question popped up on the screen.

"Did he ask me?"

Followed by a still photo of the stranger kneeling in front of Mr. Simmons, offering him ... what is that, a ring?

"Yes, he asked me," was the text shown on the next slide.

"And how did I respond?" was the final question asked before the screen went dark.

Everyone in class was talking at once; everyone had an opinion. Holding his hands high, Mr. Simmons rose from his chair, calling for the class to quiet down. As he did so, some of the students noticed for the first time that he wore a ring. Could it be an engagement ring?

"Ok, listen up, please. Listen up!"

"I had an amazing summer, and I wanted to share it with you. I met someone that I love very much. We spent a month together on Fire Island, and it was the best experience I ever had. I want to continue experiencing life with the man that I love. His name is Spencer. He asked me to marry him, and I said 'Yes.' I know this might come as a surprise to some, or maybe even all of you, but I'm a proud gay man with nothing to hide or be ashamed of. I hope you'll be happy for me. For both of us."

Just then, the bell rang, signaling the end of class. Most of the students walked out, without expressing any opinion about what they had just seen and heard. At least, not directly to Mr. Simmons.

Debi, never one to hide her thoughts, proclaimed as she left the classroom, "I can't wait to talk to my mother about what happened in school today. She's going to die!"

Jason added another P.S. to the email he had written.

"Congratulations to you, to both of you. I'm proud and happy for you. I hope you get my meaning when I say I'm proud. Maybe we can talk sometime. I wonder if I can confide in you? I sort of have a secret."

Jason paused, wondering whether it was wise to send the message. Then, he made a decision and pressed SEND.

Youngmi appeared unfazed by all the commotion. Her thoughts were consumed by the boy she now thought of as "Killer."

Charles, who had fallen victim to Youngmi's taunts earlier in class, hunched his shoulders as he slunk out of the room. He had been invisible when the class began, then had one bright, shining moment as the center of attention, even if it had been negative. All he cared about was that his classmates had noticed him, some for the very first time. But by the end of class, he was once again the forgotten soul.

Timmy walked along with Jason. "Damn, what did you think about that? I didn't have any idea he was a fag. Did you?"

Jason stared straight ahead, not looking at his bestie.

"He's gay. Not a fag — gay. No big deal, really. Is it?"

Timmy stayed silent, wondering what was going on in Jason's head.

"You do realize this is 2025, don't you? What in the hell were you thinking, showing your class something like that? Are you trying to lose your job?"

Mr. Dawson, principal of the school, had called Mr. Simmons into his office as soon as he was notified about him coming out as gay to his students.

"Yes, I'm well aware. That's why I decided it's more important than ever for me to be truthful. I want them to see that gay people aren't monsters and groomers, like some in the media and in the government portray us. We're just regular people."

"But this isn't San Francisco or New York City or some sanctuary city," Mr. Dawson replied. "You're in rural New York state and the people here are conservative and ..."

Mr. Simmons cut him off.

"So you're saying that I'm only safe in some gay ghetto, where we're isolated from the rest of the population for ... for what? Why am I supposed to stay quiet about who I am just because of where I live?"

"Look, I'm not trying to do anything except remind you of reality. You can wear your rainbow glasses and try to think that the people here are going to accept an openly gay teacher, but I'm warning you, we have to be careful about how much we let people know."

"We? Did you say 'we'? Are you telling me that you're a gay man, hiding in the closet, trying to get me to join you there like I have something to be ashamed of?"

The principal stared at Mr. Simmons.

"That's ridiculous. But don't think for a minute that this is the end. Don't be surprised if the School Board decides to take action. I've seen it happen before, and that was when people weren't as vocal as they are today. Don't say I didn't warn you."

Later that evening, while Mr. Dawson was browsing profiles on the Grindr gay-dating app, he looked for someone with whom he could have a quick, but close, encounter, while wishing that things were different. He wanted to be openly gay, but he was too afraid to risk losing his position at the school. On the app, his profile was mostly empty, and the photo he displayed was a generic one of Niagara Falls. He was jealous of those who so openly and proudly displayed themselves on the app. For him, that was an impossible dream. Imagine the reaction of the locals if they knew the principal of the high school was not only gay, but actively seeking partners.

He would only meet other men who also described themselves as "discreet," feeling safer that way. He told himself that he had done his duty by warning Mr. Simmons about the possible dangers. He would do nothing more if the teacher ever needed protection from the local homophobes, who seemed to be getting more emboldened as time went on.

Chapter Two

"Come on, slowpoke! We won't be catching any rainbows if we get there too late."

Jason climbed into the passenger seat of the old pickup truck that Timmy's dad had given him when his grandfather passed away.

"Ok, but let's stop at the diner first. I didn't have time for coffee before you got here."

"Sure thing. I could use a cup, too. Your mom working today?"

"She'll be there tonight. Same as me. You'd think she'd at least give her own son time off on a Saturday night."

"Suck it up, bro," Timmy replied. "You'll get off in time to spend your tips having some fun. At least, I hope so."

Jason wasn't sure if Timmy was giving him hints or not. He talked about catching rainbows, and now he's talking about sucking.

Is Timmy thinking about life the same way I am? Jason wondered, as he crossed the parking lot of the Niagara Diner, heading inside to get the coffees.

"I got us a box of donuts too. No use starving while we're out there fishing, right?"

"I hope some of them are creme-filled. Those are my faves, along with glazed."

"You know I did. I got the usual mix."

"Good! My mouth is already watering, thinkin' about that creamy filling," Timmy said, licking his luscious lips.

He's driving me crazy with all this sex talk, Jason thought. *But, is it sex talk? Or just normal, ordinary talk about normal, ordinary things? Is it just my imagination?*

It's 2.8 miles from the diner to Devil's Hole, a short ride that the boys often took. Jason enjoyed the view of the Niagara River, flowing north towards the famous Niagara Falls, while he gulped his coffee, trying not to spill any during the bumpy ride.

Then, he had a thought. What if he did spill some of the drink on his shirt? Then he'd have an excuse to take his shirt off, right? Maybe that would set the right tone for how he hoped this day might go. In his imagination, the fishing trip would turn into a fabulously sexy scene, with him and his best friend finally giving in to their deepest desires.

But before Jason could put his plan into action, Timmy was pulling into the parking lot, driving too fast over a speed bump, causing Jason to really spill his coffee all over himself.

"Was it too hot? Did you burn yourself? Are you okay?" Timmy blurted out all at once, concerned for his buddy.

"No, I'm okay. Just wet. Damn! It's sticky, too!"

"Lucky for you, I got a spare shirt in my gym bag back there," Timmy said, pointing toward the back of the pickup. "If you don't mind wearing one of my shirts, but I gotta warn you, I already wore it, and I didn't put it in the wash for my mom yet."

Jason had a lump in his throat, and a larger lump a little lower, as he thought about wearing Timmy's unwashed shirt.

"No problem," he replied, trying to act cool, when in fact he was very, very hot. With desire.

Climbing out of the truck, Jason started to reach for his fishing gear, watching while Timmy grabbed his gym bag, reaching in and pulling out an old tee shirt.

Taking a sniff, he said, "I don't think it stinks too bad. And at least it's dry. But it's up to you. No one's forcing you to wear it."

"Give it here," Jason answered, catching the shirt as Timmy tossed it over. "Besides, what's a little stink between friends, right?"

Timmy left the question unanswered, grabbing his fishing gear and heading down the path to their favorite spot. Jason quickly donned the shirt, inhaling deeply, feeling a pleasure he had never experienced before. But he had no time to stop and enjoy it, as he hurried to walk beside his friend.

"Beautiful day today," Jason murmured, feeling the soft breeze against his skin, the warmth of the morning sun, and listening to the chirping birds tending to their business in the nearby trees.

"This right here, it's like heaven on earth to me," Timmy replied, sounding a bit more sensitive than he intended. "It'd be even more perfect if I had a good woman at my side," he whispered, winking at Jason. "Like, I know you've been seeing a lot of the Chinese chick. You get anywhere with her yet?"

"Look at that squirrel, chasing after his female. That's what I'm talking about. You know he gets some tail every night," he continued, giggling.

"You know she isn't Chinese," Jason said, more sternly than he had intended.

"But you like her. Admit it!"

Jason sighed heavily. This wasn't the conversation he wanted-ed to have, so he let it drop.

"Thanks again for the shirt. It's nice and dry. And the smell is ... well ... it does smell like you."

21

Timmy laughed loudly at the remark.

"Okay, homo. Whatever you say."

Jason wondered if this was the right time to tell Timmy his secret. He kept thinking that Timmy was dropping hints that he was as interested in Jason as Jason was in him.

Instead, he remained silent as they walked along the path to their favorite fishing spot on the river. By the time they were close enough to hear the water, Jason jumped in front of his friend, flexed his arm, and said, "Did you notice how buff I'm getting? Check out my bicep. Pretty big, huh? You wanna feel how hard it is?"

Timmy laughed, saying, "No, Jase. I don't wanna feel how hard you are. I don't swing that way, buddy."

"I didn't mean it like that, you know. I'm talking about my arm. That weight set my Mom got me is really helping me get developed. I think it'll help me impress ... the ladies."

The hesitation in his voice might have given him away, but Timmy either didn't notice or didn't care.

"No matter how hard you try, you'll never have the body of a natural athlete, like I have," Timmy boasted. With that, Timmy flexed both of his arms, showing off his bulging biceps, then he lifted his shirt and rubbed his hand over his sleek abs.

"Now, this is what the girlies go for," he said, smiling.

Jason averted his eyes, not wanting to stare for too long. He was trying to figure out if his friend wanted more from him or not. *There's only one way to find out*, he decided. *And today will be the day we either take it to the next level, or not.*

"It's really slow today. They just aren't biting," Timmy complained after an hour sitting on the boulders at the riverbank.

"At least you got two. I didn't even get a nibble yet."

"Hey, how did Spiderman get his powers?" Timmy asked, unexpectedly.

"Come on, everybody knows he got bit by a spider. A radioactive one. Why ask such a dumb question?"

"And how about that movie *Superhero*? What happened to him?" Timmy continued.

"That's the one where the kid got bitten by a radioactive dragonfly. Remember, we watched that together. Matter of fact, we watched all the Spidey movies together, too. What's your point? Are you asking me to the movies?"

Timmy was laughing. "What about *Antboy*? What happened there?"

"Yeah, I see the pattern. Boy gets bitten. Boy gets powers. You aren't gonna bite me, are you?" Jason joked.

"No, but what do you think will happen if that giant cockroach right next to your leg jumps on you and bites you? Or even worse, what if it crawls up the leg of your shorts and gets you in the ...?"

Jason let out a girlie scream and kicked at the roach, which quickly vanished under a nearby rock.

"Why didn't you warn me right away?" Jason asked, laughing almost as hard as Timmy.

"Because I was thinking you might get a superpower, and that would be so cool," Timmy replied.

"You wanted me to turn into Roachman? What kind of powers would I get from that?"

"No, dope. Not Roachman. You'd be Cockman! The dude with the biggest cock in the universe. Just think how you could please all the ladies with something like that!"

Jason laughed even more, while Timmy was rolling from side to side, in a fit of youthful laughter.

Just what I want. To please all the ladies, Jason thought to himself. If only Timmy knew what he really wanted.

Timmy stood and stretched, then pulled his tee shirt over his head, exposing his broad chest and shoulders. Without a word, he kicked off his Nikes, dropped his shorts, and adjusted his white boxers, before taking a leap from the boulder into the little cove off to the side of the rushing river.

Both boys liked to swim in this little area, safe from the currents. They knew it could be dangerous to get caught in the river and possibly get swept over the Falls.

The sight of Timmy, shaking his hair as he came up from below the water, brought a smile to Jason's face.

"Come on in! It's just a little cold," Timmy called, laughing.

Jason didn't even need the invitation. He was already on his feet, stripping down to his white, clingy briefs, and jumping into the water, splashing playfully.

They spent a few minutes play-fighting, pushing, shoving, splashing, laughing with the sheer joy of the moment. Timmy was the first to climb back on the boulder, with Jason following closely behind.

"Ahhh, now that sun feels so good, doesn't it?" Timmy asked.

"Yep. It feels good, and it makes you look so pretty."
"What?"
"I mean, it feels pretty good. Right? Feels pretty good."
"No, that isn't what you said, Jase."

Timmy looked at his friend sternly. "What's gotten into you lately? You're acting all funny. It's weird."

Jason took a deep breath. Though he had imagined this scene a thousand times, and practiced all sorts of romantic lines to try to start this conversation with Timmy, he had never thought to begin by telling him that he thought he was "pretty."

But now that it was done, he didn't want to back down, or he might never know the truth about how Timmy felt about him.

"I have something to tell you, TJ."

It was a rare occasion when Jason would call his friend "TJ," using his first two initials, standing for Timothy John.

Timmy looked down and away, not wanting to meet Jason's eyes, unsure of what to expect.

"I don't know any other way to say this, so I'm just gonna say it real plain and simple. I like you. I like you in a way that maybe I shouldn't, but I do. And I'm hoping that you might like me, too. Not just as friends, but as ..."

"Holy hell!" Timmy muttered. "All these years, I thought we were the best friends any two guys could possibly be. And now you're telling me that you wanna ... you wanna ... do stuff with me? Like sex stuff? Hell no, you got the wrong idea. I'm not like that. I never thought of you like that. Like, never, never, never!"

Jason started to cry, very softly, desperate to hide his shame.

"And if you ever tell anybody some lie that I led you on or anything, I'll beat you so hard you'll wish you were dead!"

Every word hit Jason like a rock, each word pushing him deeper and deeper into a state of despair.

"I'm sorry!" Jason said, reaching for Timmy's hand. But Timmy turned away, refusing to be touched, getting dressed quickly.

"Come on. I'll give you a ride back home, but only because I don't want to leave you stranded. After that, we're finished. You hear me? Finished!"

Timmy was already halfway up the path back to the car by the time Jason had gotten dressed. Meekly, he followed the boy that he loved, feeling overwhelmed by what had just happened.

Before reaching the truck, suddenly, a squawk and a splash caused Jason to glance behind him. He caught a glimpse of an eagle swooping down to capture a salmon, then soaring high into the sky with its prize.

Almost in a panic, Jason caught his breath. For the moment, he knew he was trapped, in a cage of his own making. No soaring eagle was holding him captive; it was his own feelings. Now he'll be forced to fly solo, a future so bleak he couldn't comprehend what it meant.

What am I supposed to do now? he wondered.
The ride back was awkwardly silent.

"Hey Cupcake, you're home early. No luck fishing?"

"Mom, can we talk about it later? I think I wanna go up and take a nap."

"Ok, sweetie. I'll call you in time to get ready for work. We have a special guest coming to the diner tonight. And whose shirt is that? Timmy's?"

"I'll tell you all about it later. I just need some time to think. By myself."

He knew if he stood there one more minute, he'd burst into tears, so Jason turned away from his mother and hurried up to his bedroom, two steps at a time.

Lying in bed, eyes tightly closed, the scene outside his house was on constant replay in his mind.

"Get outta my truck, faggot," were the exact words that Timmy had spat at him.

"Get outta my truck, faggot!"

The words hurt more every time Jason thought about them.

"Get outta my truck, faggot!"

It was like he was being stoned to death, his heart breaking with every hateful word being thrown at him.

"GET OUTTA MY TRUCK, FAGGOT!"

Jason buried his face in his pillow, screaming in agony, terrified at the thought of being without Timmy forever.

Two hours later, he was awakened by his mother's call. "Let's go, sweetie pie. Unless you want to walk, we're leaving in two."

Glancing at himself in the mirror, Jason decided that his eyes weren't really that red and swollen as to be noticeable. He ran his fingers through his hair, trying to make himself look presentable, when in reality, his beauty needed no enhancements. Others saw what Jason could not. He was extraordinarily beautiful.

"Let's go. I'm ready, Mom."

"Oh Cupcake, what's wrong?" his mom asked as they headed for the highway. "Did you and Timmy have a fight or something?"

Jason didn't want to talk about it, so he remained silent.

"You know, dear, Timmy's a nice boy, but ..."

Jason interrupted. "No, we didn't have a fight. But we might not be seeing too much of each other. I think he's gonna be busy with his new girlfriend."

"Timmy has a girlfriend? Really? I always thought he might be gay, to be honest with you."

His mother's comment made Jason laugh for the first time since he'd been with Timmy earlier in the day.

"No, Mom. I'm pretty sure he isn't gay."

They walked together into the diner.

Katrina Masters, owner of the Niagara Diner, also worked at the front as a hostess, greeting and seating the guests, many of whom were local regulars. However, tonight she had been notified to expect the owner of the new AI technology center to be there for dinner. The ZEUS Universal Group, a world leader in the development of artificial intelligence and robotics, was in the process of completing their new US headquarters in Niagara, after being granted a variance to use hydroelectric power from the Falls for their immense power needs.

The owner, a billionaire from Greece named Zeus Vasiliadis, was staying in a nearby villa that he was renting from a celebrity, who occasionally used the place as a vacation spot.

He was rarely seen in town, but he had grown bored with the isolation here, so he decided to venture out for a night, accompanied by his wife, a former model, much younger than her husband.

Katrina was unsure what to expect during a visit from a billionaire, so she decided to conduct business as usual. No special arrangements. No special menu items, other than the normal daily specials already printed on the menus.

"Maybe he just wants a good, old-fashioned cheeseburger," she said to one of the waitresses, as they both peered out the large window, waiting for the arrival of Zeus.

They laughed, wondering if the evening would really be that simple.

He looks more regal in person, Katrina thought, when Zeus and his wife finally arrived, entering the front door by themselves. No entourage. No bodyguards.

Then she noticed that a second Rolls Royce limo pulled up and parked behind the one that had carried the billionaire couple. Two figures emerged from the first car, with four more leaving the second vehicle, taking their positions around the diner.

Clearly, the first impression was a mistaken one. The couple never traveled without plenty of security nearby.

"Table for two, please," were the first words from Zeus. "At your best table." That second sentence was more of a command than a request.

"Of course. Welcome to The Niagara Diner, Mr. Valium-topolis."

Zeus laughed.

"Oh my dear, you are so fabulously funny. Darling, write that one down," he said, addressing his wife. "Valiumtopolis. What a delicious mispronunciation of my name. And more than a little accurate, I might add," he said, winking at Katrina, as she guided them to their seats.

It was no accident that Katrina seated them in the area where her son, Jason, would be their waiter. She knew that she could count on him to be prompt and courteous.

"Ignore all your other tables until they're finished," she whispered to Jason, as he started to approach the table with glasses of fresh spring water. "The girls will pick up the slack. I want you to give those guests all your attention."

Nodding, Jason understood the assignment.

"Good evening, Sir and Madam," Jason began. "I'll be your server this evening."

Of course, this isn't the typical treatment that Jason would give a regular customer. But nothing about this couple was regular.

Zeus was dressed impeccably in a designer suit, and his wife looked like she was ready to attend a fashion show in New York City. Or Paris. Or Milan. Wherever the super-rich went to see the latest in fashion trends. Jason didn't know anything about those scenes in real life, but that was his first impression of the glamorous couple.

"No need for a menu," Zeus announced, in a commanding voice that was almost too loud for the nearly empty diner.

"The wife is on a diet, since she has strayed over her allowed weight. She'll have a small garden salad, with no dressing, a cup of vegetable soup, one half of a baked trout, and for dessert, give her a small bowl of blueberries. Will there be any problem with that order, boy?"

"Not at all, Sir. And my name's Jason. I'm the son of the owner."

Zeus ignored the boy, as if he hadn't spoken a word.

"I'll have the bacon cheeseburger, with all the trimmings, a double order of fries and a bottled water. Make that two waters. One's for the wife, too. I'll decide on dessert after the meal."

With that, he waved Jason off, treating him exactly as he would treat any servant.

Handing the order to the cook, Jason hurried over to his mom.

"You won't believe it. He calls his wife 'the wife,' like she isn't even a real person. Plus, he ordered her food without asking what she wanted or letting her order on her own. And I guess he's starving her to death 'cause she gained an extra ounce."

Katrina could hear the anger in her son's voice.

"Remember, none of that is our business," she reminded Jason. "They're here to eat. We're here to give them what they want."

While Jason was walking away from their table, Zeus looked in his direction for the first time.

"That boy does have some nice buns. I wouldn't mind eating a cheeseburger off those," he said to his wife quietly.

Pursing her lips, she said, "Of course, darling. Whatever you want. Just like you always have it."

"Talk like that and I'm going to cancel the order for your blueberry dessert," he replied, bringing the conversation to an abrupt end.

While waiting for their order, the couple sat silently. Zeus never took his eyes off his phone, while his wife stared blankly ahead. She understood that she was little more than a decorative object, mostly present so the billionaire could impress others that he had the power to always have a beautiful female at his side, ready to obey his every command.

Anyone who felt sorry for her plight was misguided, not understanding that she had been more than willing to sacrifice her soul for the empty trappings of a glamorous lifestyle.

It was only as Jason reached down to present the garden salad to his wife that Zeus took a glance in his direction — and was immediately captivated by the sight.

How does one describe beauty that's almost supernatural, beyond the comprehension of most mortals? That was the first thought that crossed the mind of Zeus.

It's quite possible that this boy is what I've been looking for, he thought. *I need to tell the others, but words won't be sufficient to convince them. His beauty is indescribable.*

"Stand still," he commanded, then took several photos with his phone, never asking for permission. Switching to video mode, he told Jason, "Walk over there, about three feet away. Then turn slowly. I want to capture every inch of you."

When a billionaire customer gives instructions to a high school boy working as a waiter at his mother's diner, what does the boy do? He obeys without question, of course.

Jason recognized the power dynamic, even if he would be unable to describe it. And if he was being perfectly honest, he enjoyed the unexpected attention from the rich, older man. He sensed no danger, since the man was with his wife. Jason made the natural assumption that this was a normal couple, who just happened to have a lot of money.

How wrong could that first impression be?

Zeus and his wife didn't spend much time at the diner. Before leaving, Zeus placed a crisp $100 bill on the table as a tip. He wanted to get back to his office to speak with his closest advisers.

"Will the boy there be back working tomorrow night?" he asked Katrina.

"Sir, the boy you're referring to is my son, Jason."

Ignoring her remark, Zeus said, "I'll be back here again tomorrow evening, with some of my closest advisors. Make sure the boy is here. They need to see him in the flesh to believe it and to make an evaluation."

He exited quickly, seeming to forget that his wife was still seated at the table. When he reached the car, he sent one of the men inside to fetch her.

"And tell her to bring me a couple of those brownies I saw on the dessert tray. They look divine, and I need something for my sweet tooth."

Katrina and Jason stood, watching them depart, wondering what the hell had just happened.

"Dad, can I get a new rifle for my birthday?"

"Do you have anything particular in mind, Charlie?"

"Not really. But I want something powerful. I want to go bear hunting this year, so I need something that'll bring down a bear with one shot."

"Let's go to Wally's tomorrow. His shop has the best selection around here. That okay with you?"

"Sure, Dad. I wanna be prepared."

"That's right. That's what I always tell you. Be prepared for anything, because you never know what danger you might face."

"I remember. And speaking of danger, maybe I could use a new pistol, too. I might need one if a snake crosses my path on one of my hunting trips."

"Now you're talking," his dad replied. "And this isn't just for hunting trips. I hope you won't forget that. You know, with that new factory they just built; you see all the strangers in town now. They don't look like us. They don't act like us. They don't know our ways. And they can't be trusted, you hear me, Charlie?"

"You're right, Dad. I don't trust strangers. I think a lot of them look like illegals, anyway."

"That's right. They look illegal. We gotta be prepared."

Charlie went down to the basement to clean some of the guns in his collection, as his dad turned his attention back to the TV news, warning about a caravan of illegals heading for the US border. The news scared Charlie's dad, even though the southern border was literally thousands of miles away.

He wants to be prepared for the war that he's sure is approaching. He's preparing his son to fight by his side.

A normal Saturday night after work for Jason would be to hang out with Timmy. Not this night, though. He wasn't sure if their friendship could ever be restored, but he knows it's too soon to try anything yet.

So, with a $100 tip in his pocket, feeling like he had money to burn, he considered his choices. He decided to go out, wanting to be around other people, even if they're strangers. He knew he didn't want to spend a Saturday night sulking alone at home.

"Mom, can I use the car? I wanna go over to Clifton Hill."

"Oh, Cupcake, I don't know. You just got your learner's permit a few days ago, and you want to break the rules already?"

Jason gave his mother his biggest smile.

"You know this smile can get me out of any trouble. Works every time," he said, winking at her.

"Yeah, like you're trying to use your charm on me right now," Katrina laughed, looking for her keys.

"If you do get in any trouble, or have to pay a fine, that's gonna be on you. I don't have money to waste on teenage nonsense," she said, trying to act the part of the stern mother.

She knew what he said was true, though. That boy could charm the pants off anyone, male or female. No border crossing guard would deny him entry. Jason was certain of that.

"Thanks, Mom!"

"And be quiet coming back in the house. You know I need my beauty sleep," she called after him, but he was already out the door, eager for a night of adventure.

Chapter Three

As he waited for the small line of cars in front of him to cross the border, Jason enjoyed the view of the Niagara SkyWheel, towering 53.3 meters (175 feet) into the Canadian sky. He remembered the fun of riding in the gondolas, enjoying the spectacular views. His one wish was that Timmy would have come along for the fun. But he hoped that he and Timmy might still be friends, and that they could enjoy the park some other time. He'd worry about that later. For now, he just wanted to forget about the weirdness of the day, the fight with Timmy, and the strange encounter with the billionaire at the diner and have some teenage fun.

The car directly in front of him was stopped, and it looked like there was some issue with the border guards. That car was directed off to the side, while the officers investigated.

Luckily for Jason, that meant he was waved through, with no one even checking his ID. He smiled at his luck as he pulled into the parking lot and headed onto the promenade.

People-watching was at the top of the agenda for the evening. He was in no hurry to enter any of the gift shops, the wax museum, the haunted house, or even the video arcades. Maybe he could find someone to keep him company and have some fun.

"Hey, Killer!" came the call from a nearby park bench.

Three or four guys turned to see who was calling.

"Damn, how many killers do you think are walking the streets here?" laughed her companion.

"Not you!" she scolded one of the teen boys staring at her. "The other killer!" she laughed, pointing in Jason's direction. But he hadn't heard her, so she ran over and grabbed him around the waist.

"There's my guy!" she said. "I didn't expect to see you here tonight."

"It was a last-minute decision, Mimi. I just got here."

Grabbing his hand, she led Jason over to the bench, where she sat down next to someone Jason had never seen before.

"I didn't know you were here with someone. Sorry, am I interrupting?"

Before either of them could answer, Jason blurted out, "I don't want to sound silly or stupid, or even racist, but I have to say ..."

He paused.

"Go ahead, spit it out. As soon as a white guy says he doesn't want to sound racist, we know what's coming next. Something racist," the boy said, folding his arms across his chest.

"No, don't start like that. I'm serious. I know that most racists will say things like, 'They all look alike,' or something else ignorant, but when I look at the two of you, well, will you hate me if I say that you look alike?"

Youngmi and her companion looked at each other, then started laughing.

"Jason, we're not laughing at what you said, and we won't think you're racist. I want you to meet Youngsoo. He's my brother."

"I'm also her twin," the boy added, still laughing at a high pitch.

The relief on Jason's face was clearly visible. His first thought was that Youngmi, whom he had started calling Mimi, was with someone who might be her boyfriend. After all, they had only known each other for a few days, and there was still much for Jason to learn about her.

He took a moment to look closely at both of them.

My god, she's gorgeous, he thought. *But her brother, somehow, was even more beautiful than her.*

He forced his eyes away from him, to focus his attention on Mimi.

"You're twins! How awesome. That means you'll both have a friend for life!"

"And that makes you Gemini, in the true meaning of the word. Is that your sign?" Jason continued.

"You believe in astrology?" Youngmi asked, not answering the question.

"I don't take it seriously, or I should say, not too seriously. But I do check my horoscope every day. Doesn't everybody?"

"I don't know," Youngsoo said.

"I had a good one today. It said, 'Avoid grief by traveling the solitary path.'"

"Sounds straight out of a fortune cookie to me," Youngsoo said.

They all laughed, and Youngsoo, who rarely, if ever, hid his thoughts, said what was on his mind.

"My sister told me she met a cute boy on the first day of school, but she didn't tell me you were hot. As in sexy hot!" Youngsoo said, winking at Jason, looking him up and down.

"Girl, you always get the cutest ones!" he said to his sister, gently elbowing her.

That wasn't the reaction Jason had expected, but he wasn't quite sure what to think about those remarks.

"Who wants ice cream?" Jason asked, switching the subject to give himself some time to figure this out.

"Come on. My treat!"

Jason led the way to a nearby refreshment stand.

"I want a vanilla popsicle to suck on. Yes, I definitely have a taste for a vanilla popsicle tonight," Youngsoo said, looking directly at Jason. "Do you like to suck on popsicles, Jason?"

"Stop teasing him!" Mimi admonished. "If he blushes any more, he's gonna pop an artery, and I won't have anyone to pay for my ice cream," she joked.

"I think Jason might want to get a frozen banana. Maybe chocolate-covered? Doesn't that sound tasty?" Youngsoo said. "Sir, do you serve frozen bananas here?" he asked the teen behind the counter.

"Hmmm, I can play this game," Jason told his new friend, eager to join in on the fun.

"Sir, never mind my silly friend there. But we do want a vanilla popsicle for him. Extra-long and extra-wide, if you have them. Oh, and if they have some creamy filling inside, all the better. If you have them, then he'll want two of them."

"Boy, he got you good!" Mimi said, laughing so hard she doubled over.

The young guy behind the counter decided to go along with the jokes.

"We don't have any of those, but I can give him a vanilla soft serve. Just wish there was some way I could harden it up for him," he said, bringing the entire group to more laughter.

"Hey! If you freaks could stop talking about your dicks for just a minute, maybe somebody can actually place an order. I'm starving back here!"

The group turned and saw a young Black boy, about eleven years old, clutching his money, looking annoyed.

"We're not talking about di ..."

Youngmi cut Jason off mid-word.

"Step up, young man, you can go ahead of us," she said, pointing him toward the front of the line.

"Thank you, and it's nice to see one of you has some manners," he scoffed.

As the younger boy ordered, Jason silently indicated to the server that he would pay for the kid's ice cream.

"Hey kid, this is your lucky day. You're customer number one-thousand, so this one's on the house," he said, handing a cone to the boy.

"See?" the kid said scornfully to the group. "You could've been the thousandth customer, but all your sex jokes cost you some free ice cream!" Then, he skipped off to join his parents and tell them about his good fortune.

"Oh snap! He told us, didn't he?" Youngsoo said, barely able to talk through his giggles.

The trio decided to settle for Orange Creamsicles, enjoying the tasty treats as they made their way toward the line for the SkyWheel, which, thankfully, was moving fairly quickly.

"You never told me if you two are Geminis," Jason reminded them.

"It's funny you ask, because we are," Mimi replied. "We were born on June 1. I don't pay attention to astrology, but maybe I should, especially if I have a boyfriend who's interested in it."

"And you're Aquarius, right?" Youngsoo asked.

"Why would you guess that? I haven't told you my birthday," Jason replied.

"Well, my dad told me."

Youngsoo realized his mistake too late.

"Your dad? Why would he know my astrological sign, and why would he tell you about it?"

Trying to correct his error, Youngsoo stuttered his reply.

"You know how fathers are. He probably did a background check on you when he heard you and Mimi were hanging out. And ... and ... he told me ... I don't know why he told me, but he did. Just crazy conversation, I guess."

Jason's suspicions were aroused, but not enough to be alarmed.

"But I never told Daddy anything about Jason. Why would he do a background check? Which does sound like something he would do, by the way, but not until he thinks I'm getting serious about someone."

"Oh, look!" Youngsoo said, gesturing at his phone. It says that Gemini and Aquarius are compatible signs. That's good, isn't it? Maybe a romance will be blossoming soon!"

Youngsoo hoped that was enough to make Jason forget about his dad.

"What else does it say about Geminis? I don't know much about your sign," Jason asked.

"Well, it says that we're smart, passionate, and dynamic. And apparently, we're characterized by Castor and Pollux, who are twin brothers in Greek mythology. However, even though they're twins, Castor was the mortal son of the King of Sparta, while Pollux was the divine son of Zeus. Their mother was Leda, and get this ... Zeus transformed into a swan to seduce Leda."

"That would make you more like Castor, the mortal one," Youngsoo told his sister. "I'm much more like the divine one. But of course, since you're a girl, you're going to play the lesser role. This story is about identical, not fraternal twins," he went on to say, never missing an opportunity to remind his sister of what he considered to be her lower status.

"But everyone already knows this story," Youngsoo said.

"I never heard anything about that," Jason corrected him. "So in this story, a human female mated with a swan who was actually the king of the gods in disguise? That's weird. I mean, really, really weird."

"It's a myth. A way to tell a story. It's really about people having two different sides. Like good and evil," Mimi continued. "And get this, it says here that Gemini and Aquarius are soulmates!"

"At least that part isn't creepy, like the other part of the story."

"There's more about Geminis. We are emotionally intelligent, energetic, and quick-witted."

"I like what I'm hearing. Especially the part about being soulmates," Jason said, taking a chance and winking at Youngsoo. He didn't think he'd have the same reaction to an advance as Timmy had. But he wasn't yet ready to say anything directly sexual to him.

It was their turn to enter the gondola to ride the SkyWheel, a new experience for the twins, but a favorite activity for Jason. Since the group behind them totaled six, which was beyond the capacity of the car, the three of them had the cabin all to themselves.

Jason let the twins enter the car first, so they could sit on the side that offered the best views. Mimi sat down, with her brother across from her, meaning Jason had to make a choice. Youngsoo tried to hide his disappointment when Jason sat next to Mimi, casually wrapping his arm around her shoulders.

As expected, both Youngsoo and Youngmi were enchanted by the magnificent views. At night, the Falls are illuminated, making the scenery even more enchanting.

"Oh look, there's the volcano exploding!" Youngsoo called out, watching as the lava flowed from the artificial volcano located amidst the Dinosaur Adventure miniature golf course below.

He was busy snapping photos, while Mimi used her phone to shoot some vids.

"That's some camera. You a pro?" Jason asked.

"Photography's my passion, actually. I want to be a pro someday, but I'm not there yet," came the reply.

"Want me to take a few shots of you and my sister for your Insta?"

"Sure, I'd love to have some photos. But I don't use Instagram."

"What? No Insta? You must be joking. You were made for Instagram. With your looks, you'd be a major player," Youngmi said.

"I don't do much on social media. I keep a low profile," Jason answered.

"But why?" said her brother. "I thought all Americans wanted to be influencers."

"I guess I'm not like most Americans, then. All I do on my socials is post some vids of Smiley Myrus and Polly Darton."

"Who?" the twins asked in unison.

"I'll tell you about them after the ride. For now, let's just enjoy the sights."

As he said that, Jason was looking directly at Youngsoo. Yes, he was enjoying the sight of that beautiful boy. Youngsoo was not unaware of the attention, and he felt like he was glowing.

At about the midpoint of the ride, which lasted for a little over 10 minutes, Youngsoo, pointing at his sister, said, "You know, if we didn't have the third wheel of the tricycle here, we could be re-enacting the Ferris Wheel scene from *Love, Simon*."

"What's that? A TV show?"

"No, silly," Youngmi replied. "My brother is talking about a scene in a movie where a cute, gay high school kid meets his online love interest, who just happens to be another cute, gay high school kid. And they meet for the first time on a Ferris wheel."

"Ohhhh!"

Jason said nothing.

"You never saw it? Maybe we could watch it sometime. Like, together," Youngsoo said softly, hoping Jason would notice the romantic lilt in his voice.

Youngmi rolled her eyes. "Stop being such a romance drama queen! We don't even know if Jason is gay or straight. And I'm beginning to think that maybe Jason isn't sure of it himself," she said, shaking herself loose from Jason's grasp and moving away from him.

Awkward.

The ride couldn't stop soon enough for Jason. He didn't want to have this conversation. Not here. Not now.

Stepping off the ride, he remembered.

"Oh look. Here's Smiley Myrus and Polly Darton. Aren't they adorable?"

Both of the twins enjoyed the video of the two French Bull-dogs, shown having a tug-of-war and then running around, chasing each other.

"But why those names? Smiley and Polly?" Youngmi asked.

Jason began to sing "Flowers," quickly joined by the other two, who both knew the lyrics.

"Oh, I get it now. Smiley Myrus for Miley Cyrus. That's clever," she said, smiling.

"But who's Polly Darton?"

Jason used his phone to access the song "Jolene" by Dolly Parton, but neither of the twins knew the song.

"There's some connection between Miley Cyrus and Dolly Parton. I think maybe Miley is her granddaughter or some-thing like that. Anyway, that's why I named my Frenchies after them. One for Miley and one for Dolly."

"Cute," said Youngsoo. "But I don't know. Is Polly ... or Dolly ... really all that famous?"

"Yes, she's a huge star. But she's older," Jason replied. "I think she might be at least 50 years old."

Jason's knowledge of Dolly Parton was limited, as he passed along his misinformed take on the matter. Dolly is actually the godmother of Miley Cyrus and they are distantly related, being seventh cousins, once removed. And Dolly, being born on January 19, 1946, turned 79 years old in 2025.

"I have some ideas about how to improve your social media platforms. You should get an Insta for yourself, plus a TikTok. And a separate account for the Frenchies. People salivate over pet accounts on those sites. And I'd love to be your official photographer. We could do all sorts of layouts for you, and we could dress the dogs in all kinds of really cute outfits, and ..."

"Ok, ok, hold on! Let me think about all that, okay?"

After wandering around a bit, Youngmi said, "Daddy just texted. He wants to come pick us up now." Turning to Jason, she said, "He doesn't let us stay out late. He can be strict sometimes."

"Too strict. He treats us like children," Youngsoo scoffed.

"If you want, you can let him know that I can give you a ride home. I drove over here all by myself and I could use some company for the drive back. Listening to you two squawk at each other will be sure to keep me awake," he joked.

"Let me check and see what Daddy says."

Mr. Kwon waited several minutes before texting his daughter back. First, he had to get back to his car in the parking lot. Instead of leaving for home after dropping off his children, he had parked and had been surreptitiously following them the entire evening.

This Korean father, who had just relocated his family to the United States, was not about to let them wander around without his direct supervision. He felt no guilt, though he made sure that his kids would not be aware of his presence. He understood teenagers and their need to feel independent, even if this wasn't the right time, in his opinion, for them to actually be out on their own.

"Daddy just said it's okay. But he wants Jason to come inside the house to meet him when we get home. He says he has to check him out to see if he's a suitable friend."

"No doubt," replied her brother. "He's gonna give you the Korean father treatment. Prepare yourself. Could be torture!" he joked.

"Oh, and one more thing," cautioned Youngsoo. "Do not be alarmed by the looks of our house. It does not, I repeat, it does not reflect our style at all. It's a short-term rental till Dad finds out if this new position with Zeus will be short-term or long-term."

"Zeus! Oh yes, I met him today at the diner. So much has happened today, I almost forgot all about it."

"Really? I didn't think anyone could ever forget about Zeus. That man is a titan!"

"And besides, your house probably looks just like mine. They're all the same in our neighborhood. It's almost like we're in a cult of ugly Americana!"

"That might be true," Youngmi answered. "But I learned one thing for sure tonight. I have a lot to learn about America and the culture here. I mean there. We are still in Canada, right?"

"What do you mean?' her brother asked.

"That whole thing with Smiley and Miley, and Polly and Dolly. I'm used to K-pop, but I think I have to listen to more American music. You know it's my goal to be as American as possible."

"Why?" asked Jason.

"I think American women are very free. In Korea, we are taught to be more quiet, more reserved, even somewhat submissive. In America, they can be anything they want to be."

"Wow! You do have a lot to learn."

Jason was not kidding.

As they neared the border crossing, Jason was driving, with Youngmi seated next to him. Youngsoo was in the back seat, unhappy about that, but not complaining.

"I never really asked, but do you mind if I call you Mimi instead of using your full name? It's a cool nickname, I think."

"No, I don't mind. It sounds more American, and that's what I want. No one back home ever called me anything but my name, but I'm getting used to it now."

"And what about you, being so quiet back there? You didn't fall asleep, did you?"

"No, I'm not sleeping. But what about me?" Youngsoo asked.

"Do you have a nickname? If I call Youngmi 'Mimi,' how about I call you 'SooSoo'?"

"No. Absolutely not. I do not wish to be called anything other than my proper name."

"Ok, SooSoo, don't get your Speedos all in a bunch," Jason joked.

"Maybe you didn't hear me," Youngsoo said sternly. "I am a man with a strong, powerful name. No one will take away my name. If they do, they take away my power. For me, this is no joke. Don't play with me like that or you'll regret it."

"All right already. Damn, you are a drama queen. I was just horsin' around."

"Beware of anyone who tries to change your name. That is your identity. A name change is not a small thing. If one chooses to do that for oneself, then it's fine. But no one should ever make you change your name against your will. Promise me that you will stand strong against an assault like that."

Jason was silent, wondering why Youngsoo had such a strong reaction. For Jason, it was a trivial matter, a joke.

"Nice to meet you, Mr. Kwon. I'm Jason Masters. I'm in school with your daughter. We're in the same Honors English class."

"Welcome to our home, Jason. And thank you for giving my children a ride home. They are both precious to me. Thanks for getting them here safely."

"No problem, Sir."

"Youngsoo will also be in your Honors English class. He had an unexpected delay and was unable to be there for the first day of school. But he'll be there bright and early Monday morning."

"Oh, that's great! I didn't know we'd all be in the same class."

Turning to his daughter, Mr. Kwon said, "Youngmi, I want you to go to bed. Right now. You need a good night's sleep, as you already know."

"Yes, Daddy. Good night." She kissed her father on the cheek and walked straight to her room, without a word to her brother or Jason.

"Dad, can Jason stay a little while? I'm not tired and I want to play some video games. It would be nice to have a competitor right in the room with me."

"Yes, you have my permission. You may go to your room now. I have to work on a presentation for work tomorrow, so not too much noise. Understand?"

It was more of a command than a question.

"Yes, Sir. We'll be quiet and won't disturb you."

Once inside his bedroom, Youngsoo closed the door quietly, then hopped onto the bed.

Jason stood by the door, not seeing any chairs and wondering about his next step.

"Come on, silly. I'm not gonna jump you. Sit here and get comfy. But no video games. I want to watch *Love, Simon* with you. I hope you'll love it as much as I do. I'll even supply the popcorn," he said, pointing to the microwave on a nearby shelf.

While they watched the movie, they laughed. They cried. They held hands.

Jason enjoyed that best of all. The warmth and strength he felt from Youngsoo was intoxicating.

"You do have beautiful hands," Jason said, bringing his friend's hand close to his face, inspecting every inch.

"Oh, I just noticed. They're polished!" Jason said, touching his nails.

"Of course they are, my dear. My sister and I get regular manicures and pedicures. For me, that's basic hygiene."

Youngsoo took hold of Jason's hand.

"You need professional help. Look at your nails. They're a bit ... jagged, shall we say?"

Jason had never even considered getting his nails done by a professional.

"Oh, I just had a horrid thought! If your hands look like this, I shudder at the thought of your feet!" Youngsoo's face showed mock horror. At least, Jason hoped it wasn't true horror, though he paid even less attention to his toes than he did to his fingers.

"I know! We should have a spa day together. One day soon. You are beautiful, with almost unbelievable natural beauty, but good grooming is also important. And it's never too soon to start a skincare routine. You probably spend too much time in the sun without protection. If you keep that up, you'll see your first wrinkles before you turn 25."

"Twenty-five is a long way off," Jason countered.

"We think we'll be young forever. But it never really happens that way. You'll see."

During the movie, Jason didn't mention this to his friend, but he fell in love. Not with the handsome boy sitting next to him. Not with any of the characters in the movie. Not with the actors playing the roles.

He fell in love with the idea of being gay. Of being authentic. Of being unafraid to let others know his true self. He was finding pride. It was a profound moment of self-discovery for him. He'd been fantasizing about Timmy for a long time, and had slowly started accepting himself as gay, but keeping those thoughts private. Now, he was gaining the confidence to share it with the rest of the world.

Once the movie ended, Youngsoo extended an invitation.

"If my father's asleep, we don't have to wake him. You can just sleep here, if you like," Youngsoo suggested. "But I have to warn you, I always sleep naked."

Jason's heart leaped at the thought. *Maybe tonight's the night.*

"Youngsoo, it's time for your friend to leave now," his father called.

"Damn! That man never sleeps!" Youngsoo complained.

"I guess I'll be going home then."

"One thing before you go. I have a question. Are you a virgin?"

Jason hesitated, looking down at the floor. This is always a tricky question for a 16-year-old boy, especially the virginal ones.

Youngsoo took his friend's chin in his hand, turning Jason to face him.

"Don't hesitate to answer when I ask you a question. That means you're thinking about it. Maybe you decide to answer honestly, or maybe you decide to lie. I don't like that. When I ask, you must always answer me immediately."

Ignoring the fact that many people can tell lies instantly and without blinking an eye, Jason looked directly at Youngsoo.

"Yes, I'm a virgin."

"Good! I like that you are untouched. I like that idea very much!"

"And what about you? Are you a virgin, too?"

Youngsoo hesitated this time.

"I thought we weren't allowed to think about our answers."

"No," Youngsoo replied. "You are not allowed to hesitate. That rule is for you. Not for me. You do know that people have rules for others that they don't necessarily follow themselves, right?"

Before Jason could answer, Youngsoo continued. "No, I am not a virgin. I'm an experienced man. And one day, or one night soon, I will give you the experience. And we will both enjoy it. I guarantee you that!"

Mr. Kwon was standing at the door, watching his son talking to his friend, still holding Jason's face in his hand.

"I told you once that it's time for your friend to leave. Do you expect me to tell you a second time?"

"No, Father. Jason is leaving now, as you wish."

Jason walked quietly into his house, not wanting to disturb his sleeping mother. Going into his bedroom, he saw a fresh pair of pajamas, folded neatly at the foot of the bed. His mother had left pajamas for him every night, for as long as he could remember. One of her motherly rituals.

Jason tossed the pajamas on the floor. He stripped totally naked, climbing into bed. He thought about it for just a moment before sending this text to Youngsoo:

"Sleeping naked tonight. Thinking about you."

He hit the SEND button, lying there quietly, unable to sleep.

Mid-mornings on Sunday are made for laziness, Jason was thinking, as he relaxed on his front porch. Just then, a dark-colored Range Rover pulled into his driveway. His new friends, the twins, got out of the car and headed in his direction.

"Oh my god, put that damn thing out immediately," came the command from Youngsoo, when he saw that Jason was smoking a cigarette. Without thinking, Jason followed Youngsoo's order.

"Give me the pack," Youngsoo insisted, as the twins climbed the few stairs to join Jason. Again, Jason followed the orders blindly, no questions asked.

Youngsoo twisted the pack, destroying the cigarettes inside, and placed a gift bag on the floor of the porch.

"Hey, that pack was full. You know how much they cost?"

"Do you know the cost to your body when you smoke those things?" Youngsoo replied heatedly. "Not only will they cause you to die a horrid death, but they'll also turn you into an old man, covered in wrinkles, well before your time. That last cigarette you just smoked was your last cigarette ever. Do I make myself clear?"

If Jason had time to think about it, he may have decided that Youngsoo had no authority over him. But he knew that smoking was a terrible habit, and though he believed it helped him relax, he also knew that arguing about it would be pointless.

"Yes, loud and clear," he said, surrendering himself to Youngsoo's authority.

"Never mind all that," Mimi said. "Daddy only gave us ten minutes to talk to you before we go for a drive. We're new to the area, so Daddy wants us all to be more familiar with where we're living."

"I could go along as your tour guide, if you like," Jason offered.

"No, Daddy said we were not to ask you to join us. And if you brought up the subject, we were told to politely decline. He said this is a family day, and you are not family. So, we politely decline."

Jason couldn't help but laugh. It wasn't so much what she said, but how it came out that he found amusing.

"So, why are you here, then?"

"My sister and I had a disagreement. We think it's important to know the truth. My sister likes you ... as a boyfriend. I also like you and want you ... as a boyfriend."

"We don't wish to waste time on someone that we'll never have. We're not asking you to decide between us. Maybe neither one of us will be the right person for you. But, we want to know if you're interested in getting a boyfriend, or if you would instead desire a girlfriend."

"Hmmm, so the real question is, am I gay or not, right?"

"Yes, that is the question. We just want to know which one of us might pursue you with some hope of success. The other will go pursue someone else. You get it?"

Before Jason could answer, his two girls, Smiley and Polly, came running out of the doggy door, stopping short when they saw the two strangers, then running over to them for closer inspection.

"Wow! They're beautiful!" Youngmi said. "Which one is Dolly?"

"Her name's Polly, Polly Darton," Jason corrected her. "She's the blonde one. Her color is officially called fawn. Smiley Myrus, come!"

Smiley, with her brindle coloring, bounded over to Jason, who picked her up, holding her in his lap, while Polly went back and forth between the twins.

"Maybe they'd like to check out the bag. I brought a gift for them," Youngsoo said, beaming.

"You did? That's incredible. We barely even know each other."

"Open it for them, please."

Jason started opening the bag, while Youngsoo continued, "I don't know if they wear pajamas at night. But I do know the nights are already getting cooler, and maybe they'll like these," he said, as Jason pulled out two of the cutest matching doggy jammies he'd ever seen.

"These are perfect! Just what the girls wanted! Thank you, Youngsoo. And look, the right size, too," he said, holding one set up against Smiley.

"You really like them?" Youngsoo asked hopefully. "I wasn't sure if this was too much, too soon."

"Not at all. I want to show these on TikTok today."

Mr. Kwon honked the car horn, letting his children know he was getting impatient to leave.

"Just really quick before we go. Do you have an answer for us? Which one of us has permission to be interested in you, and which one will be forced to look for a different lover?"

"That's such a strange way to put it, Mimi. But I understand what you mean. It makes perfect sense to want to know the truth."

Jason placed Smiley on the floor, stood, and walked over to the twins.

"If you asked me this question yesterday, I would not have been ready to answer. But after last night, I discovered myself."

"Last night?" Mimi asked.

"I didn't phrase that the right way," Jason explained. "There was something I always knew, but I wasn't ready to admit it, or accept it. Until last night."

Without giving anyone time to reply, Jason continued, taking hold of Youngmi's tender hand. "I was attracted to you the first time I saw you, that first day in English class. Your beauty is almost unbearable, and that day, I learned that you're smart and fearless, too. The way you stood up to that bully was intense."

Mimi was smiling at the thought of that encounter with the boy she accused of being known as the President of the Small Penis Society.

"But then I met Youngsoo and even though I thought I might have had feelings for a boy before, well, you brought it all out for me. You made a complicated decision seem so easy and simple. Because that's how it should be. Like in the movie we watched."

"*Love, Simon*" was all Youngsoo had to say.

"Yes, exactly. I saw how the boy in the movie struggled at first, but then he slowly opened up, to himself and then to everyone. His friends. Even his family."

Youngmi was already crying.

"So you asked for honesty from me. I'm going to give that to you. And I think you already know, but I want to say it out loud."

Youngsoo held his breath with anticipation.

"Yes, I am gay. I don't want a girlfriend. I want a boyfriend. And I want to see if Youngsoo and I have what it takes to become a couple. A real couple. As in, being both friends and lovers. That's what I want to find out."

Youngmi was sobbing as she turned and ran toward her father's car.

"I knew it," Youngsoo said. "Thank you for your honesty. I hope that you'll find me worthy. But I'll warn you right now. I will pursue you. I go after what I want. And I want you. I want you so much!"

Mr. Kwon leaned heavily on the horn, forcing his son to head back to their car.

"I want you! I want you! Never forget that, Jason. I want you!"

With that, he waved goodbye as he joined his family for their Sunday drive.

Chapter Four

Sunday evenings at the Niagara Diner are always hectic. Families like to go out for a treat after cooking and eating at home all week. Katrina needed space for six guests from ZEUS Universal, but she was worried about crowding them into a booth.

"Cupcake, push those two tables together and rearrange the chairs so they can have a nice, quiet conversation, if that's what they want. And close to the kitchen, but not too close. Oh dear, why am I so nervous? It's just a billionaire coming for dinner for the second night in a row. Do you think they want to buy the diner? Why did they want you to be here?"

"Mom, calm down. You're getting all worked up over nothing. He probably enjoyed the food. After eating all his fancy-shmancy meals, I bet he enjoyed the taste of real American food."

"Maybe you're right, sweetheart. But if he makes me an offer, it better be a damn good one. I've worked too hard making this place a success to just sell it off at bargain-basement prices."

"I hear you, but what does a billionaire want with a diner?" Jason asked.

"Let me look at you, Cupcake. You look so handsome," Katrina said, beaming at her son. "And what's that? You got a new necklace?"

"Oh, this," Jason said, holding the new gold chain around his neck. "It was a gift from Youngsoo. He had it delivered today by a drone. Can you believe that? A drone delivered it right to our house, hovering over the lawn and dropping the package right there. Good thing I got it before Smiley and Polly did!"

"Ok, stop right there. You got a gold chain from who? Youngsoo? Who's that? I thought you were seeing a new girl named Mimi."

"I didn't have time to bring you up-to-date. Sorry, Mom."

"We'll talk about it later, sweetie. We have customers waiting."

Before Jason walked away, Katrina took his arm.

"Just one quick question. What's that symbol on the necklace?"

"It's a lightning bolt. The gift card from Youngsoo said that good luck can strike at any time, just like lightning. And he said that I should wear it tonight for good luck."

After Jason texted Youngsoo to thank him, he suggested that Jason should wear it so it would be visible.

"Don't hide it inside your shirt. I'm sure it's going to bring you good luck. I can feel it so strongly that it has to be true," Youngsoo had texted back.

"Plus, it wouldn't hurt for you to lighten up a bit. You don't have to button your shirt all the way up. Are you trying to serve 16th-Century Puritan vibes?"

Jason had replied with a laughing emoji and agreed with the suggestions. So, for work tonight, the top three buttons of his dress shirt were left undone.

At ZEUS HQ, a meeting was about to convene in the board-room.

"Gentlemen, thank you for taking time out of your busy schedules to attend," Zeus said, speaking to a small group of his closest advisors and largest shareholders.

"As everyone here is aware, I, or should I say, we, made a fortune doing what we know best — AI and robotics. We are the clear leader in the technologies of the future."

"Today, I'm asking for your assistance in a pet project of mine," he continued. "You could call it my vanity project," he said, with a smile.

"For a long time, I've been obsessed with the idea of beauty. More specifically, eternal beauty. That's why I'm about to launch a new line of beauty and self-care products."

Hearing a few murmurs from the men seated at the table, he assured them.

"No worries. This will never take away from our core mission at ZEUS Universal. We will always focus on robotics and AI. But hear me out. The search for beauty is eternal, with huge market potential. Think about it. Men and women have been obsessed with how they look since the dawn of time. I want to capitalize on that, but with products of the highest quality."

"What stage are we at, may I ask?" interrupted one of the young men. "Research and Development? Ready to launch? Advertising blitz?"

"All good questions, Ari. But most everyone here won't have any direct connection to this project. I want your input on helping me to decide on the face of the line. I've been searching for someone truly beautiful, and while I do consider myself a good judge of what's beautiful, I want to get the opinions of others. Specifically, all of you. Why, you might ask? Well, it's because I trust your judgment."

Motioning for Kwon to come forward, Zeus continued speaking.

"Kwon has prepared a presentation about the overall project. Hopefully, it'll explain all you need to know, but feel free to ask questions. Oh, and before I forget, I want to remind you that while these products will be targeted for young, affluent people, let's not forget that there's a potential audience of millions of American conservatives, too. I know we've all seen plenty of red-hatted folks wearing horrendous amounts of bronzer, way too much eyeliner, overdone fillers, and botched Botox treatments that make them look like surprised freaks. And that's just the men!"

Everyone laughed. "That's so true," one of the men said, nodding to his companions.

"Before Kwon shows you the object of my desires," Zeus said, laughing, "he'll give you an overview of the background for the product line, which will include fragrances as well as many other beauty products. No plans for a fashion line yet, but you never know. Kwon, go ahead."

"Thank you, Mr. V." Turning his attention to the assembled group, Kwon continued, showing slides as he spoke.

"The overall product line is called IMMORTAL. Advertising will focus on the slogan: IMMORTAL by The House of Ganymede."

"Some of you may know the story of Ganymede, as told in the ancient Greek legends. Zeus, the King of the gods and the ruler of Mount Olympus, considered Ganymede, a shepherd boy from Troy, to be the most beautiful of all mortals. Zeus, the god, much like our founder here, admired beauty and sought to capture it for his own use.

Taking the form of an eagle, Zeus kidnapped Ganymede and took him to Mount Olympus, which was not all that unusual, except Zeus took things a step further with Ganymede and gave him immortality. Hence the name of the line — IMMORTAL.

Ganymede did not become a god. He was an immortal human being. As such, he was given the job of cup-bearer to Zeus and the other gods who resided on Mount Olympus. His job was to pour the wine at the meals of the gods, but he also served another purpose.

The stories vary somewhat, but it's clear that there was a sexual aspect to the relationship between Zeus and Ganymede. Some stories describe it as consensual, while others say that Zeus forced himself on the boy.

Of course, our promotional campaign will ignore this part of the story completely, if it involves the Greek story at all, which is still to be determined. We might just let the public remain in the dark about the origins of the storyline."

Zeus stood and spoke again. "Of course, this is the story as told by the ancient Greeks. Our purpose is to focus on the story of a beautiful young man, and how using our products will help the customers look, smell, and feel beautiful as well. Sexual attraction will only be an undertone, a concept that will be understood implicitly but not told explicitly. We don't want any accusations of grooming, of course. Certainly not in the current environment of American politics. Go on, Kwon."

"The campaign is about good grooming, but just not in the way that some people now define that word. We might want to consider redefining the word back to having a more positive connotation. That's something for the advertising campaign to consider," Kwon replied, before continuing to talk about the mythology.

"Again, the stories have various endings, but Ganymede had trouble with some of the gods on Olympus, as they became jealous of Zeus giving so much attention to the mortal. Hera, the wife of Zeus, was especially jealous, and she injured Ganymede, forcing him to live a life of eternal, excruciating pain. Zeus knew that the only solution was to revoke Ganymede's immortality so he could die and escape the unbearable pain. But since Zeus had promised that Ganymede would be immortal, he cast his soul into the heavens, forming the constellation called Aquarius. So, even today, Ganymede lives on in the heavens, forever pouring wine for the Greek gods.

We want to capitalize on this story, which is about immortal love, but also make it palatable for today's audience. So, a balancing act will be required."

"Thanks for that overview," Zeus said. "Now, can we hear about the person who I think has the potential to be the face of the House of Ganymede?"

Spontaneous applause broke out from the small group when Jason's face appeared on the screen.

"That's a very good sign," Zeus commented, pleased by the reaction from his advisers.

"This is Jason Masters," Kwon said. "Currently, a junior at Niagara County High School. He's 5 foot 9, 130 pounds, with blonde hair and blue eyes."

"Small for a model, isn't he?" came a comment.

"Remember, he won't be modeling clothing. Yes, those models are generally taller, but we'll focus on his face and other features, like his hands. His height and weight aren't that important," Kwon replied.

"Can we make his eyes green?" someone asked.

"We could. He could wear contacts. But we aren't building a robotic model here. I'm just describing the boy as he actually is."

"May I ask a question?"

"Of course, Ari. What is it?" answered Zeus.

"He's beautiful, no doubt. But did you consider using an AI model? We could build one to our exact specifications."

"I thought about that," Zeus replied. "But these products are for real people. People with imperfections. Those people might not like seeing our products applied to a model who isn't a real, physical person. There could be a backlash. That's why I decided to use a real person for the ad campaign."

"Good thinking," Aristotle agreed. "You're probably right."

"Let me tell you more about the boy," Kwon said, wanting to wrap up the presentation.

"Besides being a student, he also works as a waiter at his mother's diner."

"Oh my god, he's an actual cup-bearer already!"

"Yes, he is. And he was born on February 14."

"A Valentine's baby! Perfect!"

"Should he be called Cupid instead of Ganymede?" someone asked.

"No, we don't want this product line to be thought of as something just for Valentine's Day. With the name Ganymede, the story applies all year long," Zeus replied.

"He just turned 16 this year. Even better, he's an Aquarius. Talk about a candidate with a story to match our hero, Ganymede," Kwon said.

"He lives with his mother, Katrina Masters, in a single-family home. His father, who was killed fighting in Afghanistan, was originally named Giorgios Mastrogogiannis, reflecting his Greek heritage. Translating his name to English, he became George Masters."

"It's to our advantage that the boy's father is dead. That means we'll only need the signature of the mother in order to make any contract legal," Zeus said.

No one felt bothered by the cold, callous remark. They weren't thinking of Jason as a real human, a person with feelings. To them, he's a commodity, an item to be used to enrich themselves, selling products and services. The face of the brand might be Jason, or it might be someone else. Those particulars weren't especially important. Greed can easily make people blind, when all one really sees are dollar bills bouncing in front of their eyes.

"We traced the ancestry of the boy. On his father's side, he's Greek, with a bit of Ukrainian. From his mother, he gets his Irish blood."

"He's a fighter, then. It's in his nature, and we need someone with a strong spirit," remarked Zeus approvingly.

"Yes, a bit more about the family," Kwon continued. "The mother has a good credit score. No real debt, except for mortgages on the house and the diner. No criminal history was found for anyone in the family. They seem to be of generally good stock, leading simple, moral lives. Oh, and they do have pets. Two French bulldogs. Apparently, they belong to the boy."

"He has some nurturing instincts, I would say," commented Zeus.

"Yes, there are just a few more facts for me to tell you about him. He does smoke cigarettes, but I think he might be stopping. My son, who's already a friend of this fellow, is trying to instill better habits in him. It would be a bad look if anyone caught the face of the IMMORTAL line of health and beauty products out in public smoking."

"Good point. And your son is already his friend? That could prove helpful later on," Zeus added.

"True. Also, we know for a fact that the boy is a virgin. He confessed that to my son last night. And perhaps this will also be to our advantage. The boy is gay. Another confession he made to my son, just this morning."

"Thank you, Kwon. Great information. While it's interesting indeed to know that the boy is a virgin and is also gay, I doubt that his state of virginity will last very long. Not with a face like his," Zeus said, winking to the group of men, who all laughed.

"I don't know if he should be encouraged to keep his gay identity a secret before we launch the campaign, if he is chosen to be the one. That's for someone, maybe you, Zeus, to decide."

"Hmmm, we shall see. It might be a good quality. Women feel safe around gay men, and many women will be our customers, making purchases for their male companions. So, that might be an advantage. I'll consider all the angles."

Zeus took over the meeting once again.

"Gentlemen, this is what I'm asking of you. We will meet at the boy's place of employment this evening. He'll think we're there for a meal, but this is an inspection. You are my eagles, searching not for prey, but for imperfections. Be alert. Watch every move he makes. Inspect him carefully. His clothing. His grooming, or lack thereof. Imperfections can be improved, but we must be aware of them. Also, how he dresses. Does he show that he cares about how he presents himself to others? Does he keep his hands and nails clean? Are his manners acceptable? I want to know whether or not you believe that this boy will make a good impression on the customers for the IMMORTAL line of products. Is he the perfect Ganymede?

Once our meal is finished, write a report with your observations and any ideas that come to mind. Send your reports to Kwon, who will gather all the information into a final report for me.

Any questions? No? Then this meeting is adjourned."

"Mr. Zeus, welcome! I'm so pleased that you're here for a second time. I hope that means you enjoyed your food yesterday," Katrina said, greeting the billionaire and his party at the door.

Zeus didn't correct her mistake about his name. He cared little about what women thought, in general, and even less about what working women thought. To him, Katrina was like a fly buzzing about his head, something to be shooed away or, if necessary, swatted away.

However, he did have the presence of mind to at least smile wanly in her direction.

"Is the boy present?" he asked one of his associates. "Do you see him?"

As the men seated themselves, Jason approached, bringing a warm smile to Zeus's face.

"Hello, young man! I'm very happy to see you. Oh, and I notice that you're wearing one of my signature symbols. Is that in my honor?"

It took a moment for Jason to realize he was referring to his necklace, the one with the lightning bolt pendant.

"Yes, Sir. It's to honor you," Jason said to Zeus, figuring it couldn't hurt to humor the older man. "Plus, my friend who gifted it to me said it'll bring me good luck."

"Your friend is wise. And he has good taste. Assuming this friend is a boy. Or am I mistaken and the girls are giving you gifts?" Zeus asked, smiling.

"Oh no, he's a boy," Jason replied, immediately becoming insecure and wondering if he said the wrong thing. But then, he remembered the sense of pride he had felt while watching *Love, Simon* with Youngsoo.

"I don't have a girlfriend. This is a special gift from a special boy. Are you ready to order, Sir?"

Jason felt a wave of satisfaction wash over him. He resolved to never again be afraid to be true to himself. Although he hadn't actually outed himself to anyone he didn't already know, this was close.

"I'll order," Zeus said. "We'll have the cheeseburger platters, with double orders of fries. For everyone. But ask around to see what they want to drink," Zeus ordered.

There were no objections about the order from any of the team members. Although they were well-respected experts in their respective fields, they also knew when it was best not to question or show any signs of disloyalty to the CEO.

"I'd like to see if the boy can pour us some wine," Kwon said, as others quickly agreed, all of them thinking about the story of Ganymede, pouring the wine for all the gods of Mount Olympus.

"Mr. Kwon, how very nice to see you here," Jason said.

"What wine do you recommend with our cheeseburger meals?" Kwon asked. Everyone at the table, including Zeus, laughed at that.

"Red is normally the best choice with beef. May I suggest a nice New York State Cabernet Sauvignon?"

"Chief?" Kwon asked Zeus. "Shall we try a bottle to see his skills at pouring?"

Jason was unaware of any reason these men would want to watch him pour wine. He only saw it as part of his duties as their waiter, and once the order was placed, he was happy to oblige their wishes.

As Jason went about serving the meal and the drinks, the men kept their attention on him, watching every detail.

"Do you wear perfume?" one asked him. "Or is that your beautiful, natural, manly scent?"

"I love your shoes. Great choice, especially for work where you do a lot of walking. What size are those?" another asked.

"Have you ever tried wearing makeup?" When Jason gave him an odd look, Ari added, "You know, lots of men wear something just to bring out their best features. There's nothing wrong with doing that, wouldn't you agree?"

Jason thought for a moment. "Yes. I do agree. Although I haven't worn makeup myself, I don't see any reason why boys shouldn't. To be honest, I know a couple of guys in my class who would probably look a lot better if they wore some," he said, bringing a smile to the face of Zeus.

Conversations between the men and Jason continued throughout dinner. Zeus and his associates discovered that:

Yes, Jason would get his ears pierced, but has no piercings at this time.

No, Jason never thought about getting his nipples pierced.

No, Jason did not have any addictions to drugs or alcohol.

No, Jason had never had an STI.

No, Jason had never tried dressing up in his mother's clothes when he was left alone at home.

Well, maybe that one time when he did try on his mother's bra, but it was just that one time. Yes, he was quite sure it was only that one time.

Yes, Jason thinks that people should improve their appearances if possible.

"Within reason, of course," he had added. "Too much plastic surgery just makes people look fake," he said.

"When did you start shaving?" Jason was asked.

"Around 12 or 13, I guess. All the boys at school said we should start shaving as soon as we noticed any hair growing down there. They said we should all stay as smooth as poss ..."

Jason stopped when he saw the looks on the faces of the men at the table, realizing he had made a mistake.

"Oh, oh, oh, you meant shaving my face!" he said, laughing at his unintended admission. Trying to recover, he rubbed his hands along both cheeks, saying, "These cheeks don't need any shaving. I hope they never will. Soft as a baby's behind," he added, winking at the men, then turning and walking off with an exaggerated wiggle.

As dessert was being served, Mr. Kwon asked Jason, "Do you remember when President Clinton was asked a question about underwear?"

Jason's response amused the group when he said, "President Clinton? But Hillary was never elected President."

"We are showing our ages, aren't we?" Zeus said. "He didn't mean Hillary. It was her husband, Bill Clinton, who was President and they asked him if he wore briefs or boxers. I think it was in 1994 or around that time."

"1994! I'll be studying ancient history in school next year," Jason joked. But then he asked seriously, "What was his answer?" and the men laughed even more.

"He said he wore briefs."

Now it was Jason's turn to laugh. "So someone had the chance to ask the President a question and that's what they wanted to know? It seems so silly and unserious to me."

"True," Zeus replied. "But guess what? People still remember that moment. Sometimes you just don't know what will capture the imagination of the American public."

Ari added, "What we're really asking is whether you have anything in common with Bill Clinton." The table grew quiet as they waited for Jason to answer.

"Ohhh! Now I get it. You want to know what question I would ask the President if I could!" Jason said, kiddingly, adding quickly, "I'm just joking. I know what you want to know."

Looking around quickly, seeing that his mother was occupied with a customer, Jason undid his belt, opened his pants, and showed the group of men what he wore underneath.

"Now that's what I call a true dessert!" someone said, practically salivating at the sight of the fully-packed pouch of Jason's tight white briefs. After seeing the smiles of approval from the men, Jason quickly fixed his clothing, hoping no one at any other table had noticed.

That hope was quickly dashed when he saw a young man at a booth, part of a male/male couple, giving him an enthusiastic thumbs-up and a bright smile.

"Can I get that kind of service?" the guy commented, when Jason sauntered past a few minutes later.

As dinner was nearing its end, Zeus called for Jason.

"Come over here, my darling boy. You've been very gracious, entertaining us all evening. Just one last favor. Please pour one more cup of that delicious New York wine for each of us. I want to propose a toast."

Jason thought it a bit odd that Zeus referred to cups of wine rather than glasses of wine, but he thought it might be a cultural difference. He was completely unaware of the story of Zeus, kidnapping the mortal Ganymede, who then became the cup-bearer to the gods of Olympus.

"I do believe I forgot my manners and neglected to introduce all of my advisers here tonight. Jason, our beautiful waiter, please pour a cup of wine for Aristotle, who is the only actual Greek man present here besides myself," Zeus continued.

"And me. Don't forget about me," Jason added. "I'm a Greek man, too. Or mostly Greek, anyway."

"Yes, of course, my dear boy. We adore Greek males at ZEUS Universal. Perhaps you'll join us one day. Maybe one day soon," Zeus replied.

"Continue pouring for the rest of the group. That's Dionysius, Apollo, Hermes and of course, Hades."

Looking at Mr. Kwon, Jason said, "Sir, I didn't know your first name was Hades. How can that be?"

Laughing, Zeus answered, "No, those aren't their real names, except for Aristotle and myself. I give Greek names to the most important men in my business empire. Those are also the names of the main projects they lead. So, Kwon is the lead man on my Hades project, which is top-secret. If you ever find out what he really does for my company, we'd have to kill you," he added with a wink and a smile.

Jason hoped that Zeus was kidding, though he also decided that he'd never ask Youngsoo what his father does at work.

Once the wine had been poured, Zeus stood and raised his glass. All the men at the table rose and did the same.

"To Jason. A very fine young man, or at least, so it seems. Just looking at him brings me extreme pleasure. Perhaps he will become part of our company. We need a fresh, young face. We will decide soon if he will be named as our Ganymede. Yia Mas!"

Everyone joined in, saying "Yia Mas!" before downing their wine, which is the Greek way of saying "Cheers!"

Jason, watching as the men drank their wine, heard the words "named as our Ganymede" echoing in his mind, bringing back the words of warning given by Youngsoo:

"Beware of anyone who tries to change your name. That is your identity. A name change is not a small thing. If one chooses to do that for oneself, then it's fine. But no one should ever make you change your name against your will. Promise me that you will stand strong against an assault like that."

"Mom, look what they left me!" Jason said quietly, not wanting to draw attention from the patrons and other waitstaff at the diner. "Each one of them left a hundred bucks for a tip. That's six-hundred dollars! Can you believe it?"

"Put that away. Don't tell anyone about that," Katrina replied. "What did they want you to do for that money? Were they acting weird? Did they try to ... try to ... do you think they're perverts?" she asked, breathing heavily, close to panicking.

"Calm down, Mom. No, they aren't weird or perverts or anything like that. They're just rich. Like super rich. I think it's just natural for them to be generous."

"Don't be too sure about that, Cupcake. Six-hundred is a lot of money, and men can be more pushy and bossy than you might think," she warned.

"Look what else they left," he said, handing his mother a business card. "It's from Zeus himself."

Katrina fingered the card carefully, noting the expensive texture of the paper and the embossed writing.

Turning it over, she saw what Zeus had written on the back.

"Meet me on Friday, 5 PM. My office. I might have an offer for you."

Jason could barely contain his excitement. Katrina, however, felt a sense of dread coming over her. She was suspicious of Zeus's motives and worried that her son might easily be tempted into something that might not be safe.

Later that night, Jason came out of his room, taking a seat on the sofa, next to his mother, who was crocheting a blanket to be donated to the local Veterans Center, in honor of her deceased husband.

"That's a beauty," Jason assured her. "Almost finished, right?"

"Almost, Cupcake. Wanna watch a show with me for a while?"

"Sure, Mom. What's your pleasure? A rom-com? Or the reality one where the housewives sit around bitching about their lives while they're in the lap of luxury?"

Katrina laughed. "I love those housewives. They're so ... real!" causing both of them to laugh at the absurdity of her statement.

"Just put on something. Cupcake's choice tonight," she said, smiling sweetly, continuing to work on her project.

"I want to talk to you, anyway," she continued, growing serious.

"What was going on with you and the men from ZEUS tonight?"

"It was kinda weird. Like an audition or something. I'm not sure what they were talking about, but at the end, Zeus said he was thinking about naming me as his Ganymede."

"What's a Ganymede?"

"I had to look it up. It's a moon of Jupiter. You know, the planet."

"Oh, Cupcake, I don't know much about astrology. Or is that astronomy? I get those two mixed up."

Jason laughed. "It's astronomy. The other one is when you read your horoscope each morning."

"Don't act like you don't read yours, too. Besides, since we're both born Aquarius, our horoscopes are the same every day."

"True. And guilty as charged. I like to read them, though just for fun."

"So, what do you think they mean about giving you that name?" his mother asked.

"I'm not sure, but I've been thinking about it. Like, what do I have in common with a moon? It's kind of an insult, I think. Because a moon doesn't create heat or light. It reflects it from a different source, like the sun. So if Zeus thinks I'm going to reflect his light, like he's the sun and I'm just a moon, do you think that's a compliment?"

"Well, maybe not. But at least he doesn't want to name you after a comet, or a distant galaxy. A moon is close to its planet, right?"

"Yes, that's a good point. But the other thing about a moon is that it revolves around the planet. It's a follower, not a leader."

"Maybe you can ask him to name you Mars. That's a planet. Just don't let him name you the same as that other planet with the weird name."

Jason thought for a second, naming the planets in his head.

"Oh, I get it! No, nobody will ever name me Uranus. You can bet the house on that!"

Katrina, deep in thought, ignored the joke. After a few moments of silence, Katrina added, "Why is he even talking about changing your name? Did you say something about not liking yours? Were you thinking about changing it?"

"No, nothing like that. I like my name. Jason Masters. It's a cool name."

"Yes, but remember, your father changed his name because he wanted to be more American. And besides, nobody could pronounce his last name. Not even me," she laughed.

"You could have been named Jason Mastrogogiannis," she added, pronouncing the name perfectly, contradicting herself.

"That wouldn't have been so bad, though I like the name he chose better. I have to admit that. But is there anything wrong with having your name changed?" he asked.

"I think it depends on the reason for the change. There are good reasons. And there are bad reasons."

"What would be a bad reason?"

"Well, if you're trying to evade the law, I guess. Or maybe to get away from something like paying alimony. Men try that, you know."

"Then what's a good reason?"

"Well, sweetie, some people change their names to better reflect who they truly are. I'll give you one example. You know Maria who works at the diner?"

"She changed her name?"

"No, not her. Her child. His name was Mario and now her name is Margarita. That name represents her true nature. You understand?"

Jason leaned over, placing his arm around his mom's shoulders, holding her tightly.

"Yes," he whispered. "I do understand."

Chapter Five

At 4:44 AM, Mr. Dawson, the principal of Niagara County High School, received this message on his school district email account:

Beware! This is the day of your surprise! Open your eyes to find yourselves in the realm of the dead. It is the day of justice for my enemies at Niagara High.

"Let death take my enemies by surprise; let them go down alive to the realm of the dead, for evil finds lodging among them." Psalms 55:15

At 5:07 AM on Monday, this message was sent to all members of the Niagara School District community:

A threat has been received, targeting the Niagara County High School campus. We do not believe that this is a credible threat, but due to an abundance of caution, all classes and extracurricular activities at Niagara County High School scheduled for today are canceled. The safety of our students is our highest priority.

Please note that all teachers, administrators, and other staff at Niagara County High School will report for work with a one-hour delay, in order to allow for the building to be thoroughly swept for any devices that may cause harm.

Mr. Simmons sat bolt upright in bed, having been awakened by the alert on his phone.

"Oh no! Spencer, this is awful. Even a quiet area like this gets bomb threats. At a school, no less!"

His fiancé sat up next to him, read the message and said, "Of course, the safety of students is always the priority. But a one-hour delay for you and the other teachers? Why isn't your safety also their highest concern?"

Benjamin elbowed him. "Come on, be real. They don't want to pay us one day without actual work being done. We'll probably have to sit in the library writing lesson plans, or maybe they'll force one of those god-awful professional development sessions on us. Either way, they want to make sure we aren't spending the day enjoying good times with our loved ones."

The two men kissed and fell back onto the bed. They had a few minutes for fun before they had to get up. They spent their precious time together as young lovers do, providing pleasure to the one they loved.

Youngsoo texted Jason as soon as he saw the text.

"No school today! Wanna hang?"

"Sure! Can you pick me up?"

"I'll be there around 9. See you then," Youngsoo replied.

"That's your car?" Jason exclaimed, when he saw Youngsoo exiting his Porsche 911, its brilliant Guards Red shining in the morning sun, with the black accents providing the perfect contrast.

Youngsoo didn't believe in false displays of modesty. He proudly showed off his car, wanting to impress his friend and knowing he'd succeed.

"This baby was my birthday present. From Father, of course. He knows how to spoil me, though it's true this is what I asked for."

Jason suddenly realized that the Kwon family was much richer than he had first imagined.

"I was thrilled to get a couple hundred in tips last night," Jason said, trying to brag a little, but quickly realizing that a truly rich person would not be impressed by his meager earnings.

"I'm sure you always get tipped well. Considering you're the best-looking boy working there," Youngsoo said, trying to be agreeable and complimenting Jason.

"Not like last night," Jason replied. "Zeus himself was there for dinner. For the second night in a row. Your daddy was there, too."

"I'm not Mimi," Youngsoo chastised him. "I do not call my father 'Daddy' and neither should you refer to him that way."

"Of course, you're right. But can I ask ... do you have to do anything to earn a gift like that? Like, I don't know, chores? I guess that sounds silly, but I don't know, which is why I'm asking."

Youngsoo smiled at his friend.

"All I have to do is to be a good, obedient son to my father. If he asks me to do something, I do it. And if he tells me to do something, I obey immediately. It's how I show my respect to him."

"The girls want to see you," Jason said, changing the subject. "Wanna come inside?"

"Can you bring them out here? Father told me to never enter anyone's home unless I've checked with him first, and I don't want to bother him right now."

"Sure. No problem."

A minute later, Jason came outside with Smiley Myrus and Polly Darton close at his heels.

"Let me snap a few photos of the three of you and I'll post them later today. You know, I'm going to turn you into one of the brightest stars on social media."

"You mean me and the girls. No one wants to just look at me," Jason said.

"Oh sweetie. How wrong you are about that. Just wait. You'll find out soon enough."

After some quick poses, Youngsoo asked, "Ready for a ride? I love driving this beauty. Wait till you feel the power!"

"Let's go!" Jason agreed. "That is one beautiful car. Sleek. Bold. And it was a birthday gift. I can't even believe that!"

"Father can be quite generous. To be honest with you, so can I. Speaking of which, that necklace I sent you looks perfect on you. Did it bring you good luck?"

"Maybe. I'll find out more later this week," Jason said, not wanting to give too many details in case he was being overly optimistic in his thoughts about what Zeus might have to offer to his Ganymede.

"It's the nicest jewelry I have. Thanks again. If I'm being really honest, it's the only jewelry I have," Jason added, fingering the lightning bolt dangling from his neck.

Youngsoo headed straight to Frederick's, which he had found while searching for the best men's clothing shop in the area. As they drove toward their destination, he said, "Father was very worried about that threat at school today. He didn't want us to go to public school, but I convinced him that it was a great way for Youngmi and me to socialize. But now, even I wonder if I made the right decision. Do you think we're safe?"

Jason thought for a moment. "I feel safe. I mean, I've always felt safe here. Nothing bad ever happens."

"But do you still feel safe? Even after this?"

"I trust the police to do their jobs. I'm sure they're checking the school right now. Besides, it was probably a prank, like some senior trying to get an extra day off, or maybe someone didn't study for a test or something."

"I hope you're right. Father will pull us out and get us tutors if he thinks we're in any danger. And, if I can be honest, I'd be unhappy if I didn't get to see you in school. Tomorrow, we'll have our first class together. All three of us. You, me, and my sister. It's going to be fun."

Pulling into the lot at Frederick's Finest Fashions, Youngsoo asked, "Do you like cashmere? I still have some credit left on my card for this month. I have to spend it all so Father will replenish the full amount he gives me every month."

"What are you talking about?"

"My credit card. If I don't spend the entire $20,000 every month, then he just pays the balance. Like if I spend 5 thou, he'll pay that bill, and I'm out 15 thou. Get it?"

"You get 20 Gs every month from your daddy ... I mean, from your father? I don't know how you spend that much every month."

"Well, it sounds generous, but it isn't, really. It's easy to spend that and much more when you start buying luxury brands. Sure, I can get a starter Patek Philippe for maybe 20 or 25, but the very best cost up to 2 million. That's what true luxury means; you know?"

Walking into the store, Youngsoo greeted the owner. "Frederick, my darling! What a lovely store you have here! I hope there are some nice cashmere sweaters in stock. We want to wear matching sweaters to school tomorrow. To make a statement, you know what I mean?" Youngsoo said, winking at Frederick, who was grinning broadly at the obviously rich, obviously gay young couple.

"I have a beautiful collection. Perhaps you might consider matching outfits for more than one day," Frederick suggested, expecting a very good sale from these two.

Jason didn't object to getting matching sweaters. In fact, he liked the idea. It sounded romantic, and he longed for a true romance with a guy who wouldn't want to hide his feelings.

He felt a twinge of regret that he wasn't there with Timmy, but he had to accept that Timmy was going to move on with his life, without including Jason. Youngsoo was filling the deep hole that had been carved into Jason's heart when Timmy had screamed at him just a few days ago.

He could still hear and feel the hate in Timmy's words.

"Get outta my truck, faggot!"

Pushing those thoughts aside, Jason brought himself back to the present.

"This is the softest fabric I ever felt! What color do you think suits me?"

"Yes, it's very soft. It's sensual. It kinda turns me on, you know what I mean?' Youngsoo said softly, imagining Jason wearing the cashmere ... only the cashmere, his pulse quickening at the thought of a naked, willing Jason ready to be taken for the first time.

"You'll look perfect in the baby blue, don't you think? It brings out the blue in your eyes. And look at this one in plum! Would you be okay with both of us showing up at school tomorrow wearing our plum cashmere sweaters? I want everyone to notice, and there's no way anyone will be able to ignore us in those, and they'll get what it means, too,"

Youngsoo said very quickly, the words tumbling out of his mouth in excitement.

This is what I want in a boyfriend. Someone proud to be with me. Someone who won't hide his feelings, Jason thought, trying again to push the thought of Timmy out of his mind.

"Can we get both? The blue and the plum? I love both of them so much!"

"Yes, babe. We can get both. I told you I can be generous. Now, let me show you."

"What do people around here do for fun? Youngsoo asked, after they'd gotten back in the car.

"It's a quiet area, that's for sure. We do simple things. Fishing is a favorite activity of mine. Swimming, when it's warm enough. Video games sometimes. What do you like to do?"

"Me? I like to go shopping. I spend lots of time on social media. It's important for me that people know who I am. I want lots of followers, and I always want to get plenty of likes on my posts. I spend more time indoors than outdoors, but I wouldn't mind changing that. And of course, my true passion is photography. You know I develop my own film, right?"

"Oh, I didn't know that. Very cool."

"What about partying? I would guess lots of the kids in public school get high all the time, right?"

"I'd be lying if I said 'no,' but that isn't my scene. I don't want to OD and lots of the drugs around here are laced with all kinds of additives. You know, like fentanyl. I don't wanna mess with that. Too dangerous."

"Plus, it ages you. Very bad for your skin. I take good care of my body. I forgot to mention that my spa days are the best days of the week for me," Youngsoo added. "I have an appointment for later this afternoon. Full treatment. Facial, manicure, pedicure, and of course, the best part, the massage!" he laughed. "You should come with."

Jason agreed without hesitation. He wanted to have new experiences. He also felt that it was time for him to explore new ways of looking at the world. His worldview up to now had been narrow and limited. His expectations had been that he'd probably lead a quiet, simple life, here in Niagara, and those thoughts had been sufficient, even satisfying. Until he met Youngsoo. And Zeus, of course. He was beginning to see that there was the potential for bigger and better experiences. And maybe that was a good thing.

As they drove along, Jason's thoughts were getting him excited about new possibilities in life, as he continued to talk with his new friend, mostly directing him toward the Niagara River. Suddenly, Youngsoo pulled over and stopped the car, reaching quickly for his camera case.

"Eagles! I just spotted two bald eagles. I need some photos. They are magnificent creatures!" Youngsoo said.

The two boys exited the car, scanning the skies above.

"Over there!" Jason said quietly, pointing to the two birds circling overhead.

Youngsoo appeared calm, focusing his lens and snapping photos, but his heart was beating rapidly. He had a growing appreciation for the natural beauty in this area, and he was hoping to build a wildlife and nature portfolio.

"They're doing the Daredevil Cartwheel! Watch them!" Jason whispered, captivated by the sight of the two birds engaged in flight, locking their talons together, then descending in a spiral, plummeting toward the ground, releasing themselves just before impact.

"I've never seen anything like that before," Youngsoo said, awestruck. "It's like a dance."

"More like a mating ritual," came the response. "If they're newly paired, it's a way to court a potential mate. If they've been together for a while, they're reaffirming their vows, renewing their commitment to each other."

"Amazing! It's like they have their own culture."

"Yes, and it isn't only for mated pairs. Sometimes, two males will do the Cartwheel."

"Because they're gay?"

"No, I don't think so. It's to assert dominance over a rival. Almost like they're wrestling each other on the way down."

"Maybe the females gather to watch, to see which one would make the better mate."

"I wouldn't be surprised. They want to make the right choice. Just like people," Jason agreed.

"Two more. Right there. Nesting. Look at them!" Jason continued, gesturing towards a wooded area close by. "You see them? In that tree?"

"Good eye! Like an eagle!" Youngsoo joked, turning his attention to the nesting pair and taking photos quickly.

It seemed as though the eagles were aware of the spying eyes of the humans below. The male stood on the edge of the nest, behind his mate, and spread his wings, flapping them to show his beauty and strength, but not flying off.

"Look, I think he's teaching you a lesson," Youngsoo said. "He's telling you it's time to spread your wings. Be a show-off. Be flamboyant. It's okay to show your stuff and to let people look at you with envy and admiration. And at the same time, he's being protective of the one he loves. That's a beautiful scene right there!"

Jason's heart was fluttering, listening to the advice he was being given. His attitude toward life, toward the world around him, was in the midst of a sea change. Meeting this wise, young man was having a profound effect on him. For just a moment, he thought, *could this be love?*

Before today, Jason's goals were ordinary, pedestrian. He would have gotten excited just to have a car. Any car. But if he could get better things, more expensive things, well, he was beginning to think that there isn't anything wrong with that. Isn't that the American dream?

"Have you seen the Floral Clock yet? It's beautiful, and I think the whole idea is romantic. Perfect for a walk on a day like this."

Youngsoo replied, "No, but that sounds cool. Want me to head over there now?"

"Ok, but it's over on the other side," Jason answered, referring to the Canadian side of the Falls. "Do you have your ID to cross?"

"Yes, but Father would kill me if I went over the border without getting his permission first. And I can't bother him right now. I know he has a big meeting with Zeus this morning. Can we go there some other time? Anything we can do over on this side?"

Jason thought for a minute. After a brief pause, Youngsoo continued.

"I have to say, the Canadian side seems to be where all the action is. There's a lot more going on over there. Don't Americans appreciate what they have here?"

"It's true. There's been a lot of development and tourism over there. I don't know why this side is like a ghost town. But one of my ancestors, I don't know which one, wanted to live in the States, so here we are."

"I don't know why Zeus decided to build his tech center on this side. It probably has something to do with tax breaks. Because if there's one thing I know about billionaires, it's that every decision they make is based on saving money."

"Isn't that strange?" Jason said. "You'd think they'd just spend it, since they have so much. Instead, they hoard it, like they're afraid of losing it. Weird, right?"

Jason pointed to a parking lot, and Youngsoo headed in that direction as their conversation continued.

"How's Mimi?" Jason asked, thinking it was probably impolite not to ask Youngsoo about his sister.

"She's okay. We don't really spend all that much time together."

"Why not? She's your twin. And on the first day of school, she told the class that her name means Forever Powerful. That's so cool. Does your name have a cool meaning, too?"

"My name is Youngsoo Kwon. My name also means Forever Powerful, but I have the masculine version of the name, which, by way of nature, makes me more powerful than my sister could ever be."

"Oh, I had no idea. That your names meant the same thing, I mean."

"Yes, it's true. But like I said, since I was born as a male, I have greater value in society. It's always been that way and always will be. Being a female makes my sister weak and inferior to me."

"You don't really mean that."

"Why wouldn't I? It's the truth. In Korea, women are expected to become wives, mothers, housekeepers, or similar roles. I see America becoming more like that now. For a while, there was a push for equality, but now American men are pushing their females back into the kitchen."

Jason didn't answer as they exited the car. He had been raised by a strong, working mother, and he admired her for that. He thought of the girls in his class as being equal, without ever questioning it. Youngsoo was giving him some things to consider.

Youngsoo continued talking as the two teen boys headed down the path toward their destination.

"My sister is beautiful, I think. But I am even more beautiful than her. She's strong, but I have more strength. She's also smart, but my intelligence exceeds hers. She is powerful, but in a feminine way, if you understand what I mean. On the other hand, I'm powerful in my masculinity. I am destined to have power over all women and over weak, feminine males. My Father has taught me this. He is correct. Do not underestimate me and do not fall for my sister's charms," Youngsoo warned.

Jason pondered these words from Youngsoo. He wanted to agree with him, mostly because he was attracted to him, and saw him as a potential boyfriend.

Is physical attraction enough for a relationship to last? How much do people have to agree on in order for things to work out in the long term? Certainly not everything, Jason thought.

His thoughts were interrupted as they reached their destination, ready to board the Maid of the Mist boat ride that would take them over to the Cave of the Winds.

"Let me help you with that," Youngsoo offered, helping Jason with the blue poncho, provided by the tour, that would help keep them from getting soaked by the Falls.

Youngsoo was constantly taking photos, not only of the majestic natural scenes, but also of Jason, who always looked beautiful, whether wet or dry, whether perfectly styled or with his hair wet and wild in the wind during the boat ride.

This was Youngsoo's first time on this tour, so he was surprised when the tour guide explained how the Cave of the Winds had gotten its name.

"The first two people who ever walked behind the Bridal Veil Falls into the cavern were Barry Hill White and George Sims, who decided to name it 'Aeolus Cave,' after the Greek

God of the Winds," the guide recited his lines, exactly as scripted.

"That, my darling, is an example of whitewashing history," Youngsoo said. "Do they expect us to believe that no native people ever stepped foot into the cave before the two white guys? Typical American fantasy."

Jason nodded, his face dripping wet, his hair soaked, enjoying the forces of nature as well as the companionship of a boy almost as beautiful as himself.

The tour guide continued, saying, "The first man to discover the cave, Joseph Ingraham, didn't like the name chosen by White and Sims, so he renamed it 'The Cave of the Winds.'"

"And isn't it strange that these three men are fighting over the name of the place? Doesn't it sound a little ... suspicious?" Youngsoo asked, arching his brow, feigning a limp wrist, and winking at Jason, who laughed so hard he almost fell over, slipping on the wet floor of the boat.

For the rest of the trip to the cave, Youngsoo forgot about taking photos, preferring to keep his arms wrapped tightly around Jason, feeling the warmth of his body as he protected his companion from the winds and water.

"I bet Zeus would love to hear that story about the cave being named after a Greek god. The next time you see him, you should tell him about that," Youngsoo shouted over the roar of the Falls, as the boat passed close by.

Jason was hoping for a more romantic comment, as he was feeling excited by the strength of Youngsoo's arms around him. Still, he smiled and nodded in agreement, moving closer to Youngsoo, rubbing his body against him, hoping to excite his companion as well.

Jason moaned softly when he heard Youngsoo whisper in his ear, "I can feel your heart beating rapidly, moving all the blood in your body into your most private area. Your lungs are barely able to keep up, because the thought of me, the object of your desires, is almost too much to bear."

Youngsoo's fingers lightly brushed Jason's lips, drawing the outline of the luscious flesh.

"I will have you as mine. You will surrender to me. You know this is the truth. You cannot deny it. You want me even more than I want you."

Jason's knees buckled under him at the thought of being intimate with another boy.

"Yes," was all he needed to say. It was all he could say. He was beyond words. He was trembling with desire.

"You go on with the rest of the group," Youngsoo told Jason, as the passengers began disembarking, ready for the next part of the tour. They had arrived at the Cave of the Winds, and would be following the walkway built for tourists. "I want to talk to that guy for a minute."

Jason immediately felt a rush of jealous rage.

Why am I feeling this way? It's crazy to be jealous over a boy I hardly know. But if I'm considering giving him my love, my soul, my body. Shouldn't that happen with a boy that I can trust? Why am I this upset just because he wants to talk to someone, without me present, even for just a minute?

When Jason looked back, he saw Youngsoo holding the hand of the crew member, a young man in his early 20s, with a strong, sturdy build and a brilliant smile, visible even at this distance. The man nodded enthusiastically, taking something from Youngsoo's hand and placing it into his pants pocket.

Jason was glad his face was wet, so Youngsoo might not notice his tears when he finally left the boat.

"I see why they call it the Cave of the Winds," Jason said as they made their way along the path.

"They should have called it the Wet Winds," Youngsoo replied, as they were splashed by the Bridal Veil Falls, the smallest of the Niagara Falls, though it hardly seemed that way at the moment.

Jason took hold of Youngsoo's hand, wanting to be held steady against the forces of nature that almost felt like an attack.

"This is so awesome! Feel the power! This is what it feels like to be a powerful man!" Youngsoo screamed, so he could be heard over the roar of the rushing waters.

Then, Youngsoo took hold of Jason, wrapping his strong arms around Jason's slim waist, lifting him into the air and holding him high, as if making an offering to the gods of nature.

"My ancestors follow me wherever I go," he shouted. "Listen to me, my ancestral heroes. This boy is mine, and I beg you to protect him always, as you have always protected me. We are of the same spirit. Please grant my request, ancient ones!"

Jason, who had never even thought about asking his ancestors for anything, was a little confused, but he sensed that something important had just happened. When Youngsoo placed him back on the walkway, feeling the tight grip of protection from his companion, he felt more special than he had ever felt before.

After their allotted time, Jason turned to head back to the boat, following the rest of the passengers, when Youngsoo grabbed hold of him, holding him back.

"We're not going back with them. I'm taking you on an adventure. Will you trust me?"

"Sure, I trust you, but the only place we can go is back down there."

"No, the guy on the boat told me how we can get past the barriers and go down to a secret area. I paid him for the information. Come with me. He'll do a deliberate miscount of the people who get back on board, and we'll have some time here alone. Come on, it'll be fun, and we can catch a later boat back to the car."

Jason followed as Youngsoo led him to a fenced area. They ignored the sign with the huge red letters, warning:

NO TRESPASSING!

VIOLATORS WILL BE PROSECUTED

TO THE FULL EXTENT OF THE LAW!

They followed a path that few had ever followed before, at least not in modern times.

"The dude on the boat said that people used to come down here, behind the Falls, but there was some accident, so they closed it off. The insurance costs alone would put the company out of business if they ever brought tourists down here."

"On the other side, people can take The Journey Behind the Falls. It reminds me of some scenes in the movie *Niagara*, with Marilyn Monroe and Joseph Cotten. You know, someone gets murdered in that movie, and someone else goes over the Falls."

"I do know. Father made me watch it before we moved here. I liked Marilyn very much. So beautiful, just like you," Youngsoo replied.

"But if we were over on the Canadian side, we wouldn't have the pleasure of being here all alone, right?" he continued.

They found themselves perched on a ledge, about a hundred feet behind the never-ending rush of the Falls. Both stood still, entranced by the sheer beauty of the sight before them.

"Look at all the rainbows. There must be twenty of them, all at once!" Jason said quietly, as the walls of the cave absorbed some of the sounds from the water, making it easy to speak without shouting.

"That's a sign of good luck! Come on!" Youngsoo shouted, taking Jason by the hand, leading him down a path closer to a pool of calm water below them.

"I've lived here my entire life, and I've never been here before. Unbelievable!" Jason said.

While Jason couldn't take his eyes off the beauty of the natural surroundings, Youngsoo had other thoughts on his mind. He was behind Jason, removing all of his clothes.

"I'm going in. Watch me!"

"Stop! Don't jump! It could be dangerous!"

When he turned and saw Youngsoo completely naked for the first time, Jason felt a flood of emotions.

He couldn't help but admire the sheer physical beauty of the boy in front of him. *The body of a gymnast*, he thought, *and the face of a model.*

Suddenly, he thought of Timmy, his best friend from forever, who also had an athletic body, though Timmy more closely resembled a wrestler or a running back.

"Look at my strength! Look at my power!" Youngsoo cried out, flexing his arms and showing off his huge biceps. "I can crush men with these arms! And I will. I will crush my enemies to death, no matter who tries to stop me!"

Jason didn't really hear Youngsoo's words. His attention was focused on a part of Youngsoo that he had never seen before.

He let out a sigh of desire as he imagined himself being with Youngsoo, in an intimate way.

Once again, thoughts of Timmy invaded his mind. Jason had spent hundreds, no, thousands of nights, fantasizing about being with Timmy. And now Timmy was being replaced by this beautiful young creature, really still a stranger, though Jason also wondered how well he really knew Timmy, even after all those years. After all, he had misjudged how Timmy would react. Would Youngsoo also push him away one day?

"Don't stand there gawking at me like a schoolgirl," admonished Youngsoo. "I know you like what you see. Now it's time to show me yours. Clothes off, now!"

"I don't want you to be disappointed," Jason protested.

"Let me worry about that. But I already know I'm gonna like what I see."

Jason hesitated, then obeyed, removing every article of clothing. He stood there, acting more like a frightened sparrow than a man with pride in himself, holding his folded hands in front of himself, in a vain attempt to hide his state of arousal.

"Oh, yes, you are a perfect boy!" Youngsoo said, smiling a wicked grin.

"I was pretty sure you liked me, but now I see the evidence of how much you like me," Youngsoo said, smiling at the sight of Jason's arousal. "And it's cool that you're a grower, and I do mean, you grow really big!" he added, licking his lips lasciviously.

"Are you ready to kneel before your god and worship me in the way I deserve?" Jason said, approaching Youngsoo, expecting to have his very first true sexual encounter.

"That's what you thought I brought you here for? No, you really have the wrong idea. Not only is this the wrong time and the wrong place, but you're gonna have to rethink our positions."

"But let's leave that discussion for some other time. The one thing I do know is that both of us are going to be shrinking the minute we hit that cold water," Youngsoo continued.

"I'm not getting in that water! Are you crazy?"

"I sure am! I'm a crazy teenage boy in a cave with another crazy teenage boy. And the best part, we're both naked and by ourselves, and we can act as crazy as we want!"

With that, he grabbed hold of Jason's hand, pulling him toward the edge, and then they both howled with delight as they plunged feet-first into the pool below.

The cave walls echoed for the next twenty minutes with the sounds of two boys, laughing, splashing, diving, swimming, floating, and having so much fun, just being in each other's company.

"Come on, let's go dry off," Youngsoo said, climbing back up to the top of the ledge.

Jason hoped that Youngsoo might change his mind, and that this would be the time it would happen, but Youngsoo got dressed, having no intention of making any sex moves. He had already decided that their first time would be in a much more luxurious setting. Not in a cold, wet cave, under a waterfall. Though it was indeed a beautiful setting, it didn't lend itself to a lengthy encounter, which is how Youngsoo wanted it to be.

After they both dressed, Youngsoo indicated that Jason should sit next to him.

"We have a few minutes before we have to go. Let's talk."

"What do you want to talk about?" Jason asked.

"The future," came Youngsoo's reply.

"Ok, I'll go first. A guidance counselor at school once asked me this question. Where do you expect to be in five years? Have you ever thought that far ahead?" Jason asked.

Youngsoo didn't hesitate to answer.

"My future is already set. I've seen it clearly many times. I'm 16 years old now. In five years, I'll be twenty-one. And at that age, I'll be one of the top lieutenants at ZEUS Universal. I'll already have a Greek name, bestowed on me by Zeus himself. I'll be the man in charge of one or more of his companies."

"You're very sure of yourself."

"Yes, I'm ambitious. But I'm not done yet. In five more years, I'll be the head of ZEUS Universal. I'll own everything that Zeus owns now, and even more. I'll be rich and powerful beyond imagination."

"How's that possible? Won't Zeus stop you?"

"He won't be able to stop me, because I'm going to kill him. And I'll do it in front of all his advisers, including my own father. They will all submit to my power and domination over them. This is my destiny. I'm certain of it and I'm going to make it happen."

"Wow!" was all Jason could think to say, completely taken aback by Youngsoo's vision of the future.

"And I know your future, too," Youngsoo continued.

"You can't possibly know what will happen to me. You hardly know me. You don't know what I want."

"What you want is immaterial. It's your destiny, whether you want it or not. In you, I see someone very special. I knew it the minute I first saw you, the night we rode the SkyWheel. You, my darling, have a very bright future ahead. You're going to be super-rich, super-famous, a megastar. And, you are among the most rare of the stars, destined for immortality."

Jason was speechless as Youngsoo once more took his hand, leading him back to the path, walking to the dock where they boarded the tour boat, already waiting for the return of the next load of tourists.

The same crew member who had allowed them to stay back from the earlier group greeted them as they boarded.

"I'm glad you boys made it back safe. It can be tricky down there. But did you like it?"

"We had the best time!" Jason assured him.

"Me and my friend go down there to party sometimes. Let me know if you ever wanna join us. We get kinda wild sometimes," he said, winking at Youngsoo.

"And speaking of wild," he continued, "wait till you see this group we have on board now. They've been singing and dancing the entire trip. And they're all seniors. I hope to have that much energy when I get old!"

Jason and Youngsoo stood at the side of the boat, enjoying one last look at the Falls, brilliantly reflecting the setting sun. Then they turned their attention to the group onboard. They had just finished a song, when one of them, sounding like a professional, began the opening line to "Aquarius/Let the Sunshine In," made most famous by The 5th Dimension.

"Oh my god, they're singing about you. You are Aquarius. You know that, right? You're the brightest star in the constellation of Aquarius. How did they know?" Youngsoo asked in amazement.

One of the seniors came over to the two boys.

"Can I interest you in a brownie? It's Rosemary's special recipe, and we only share them with people we know are special, like we are."

"Sure!" Jason said, reaching for one.

"Oh, I just want to be sure you know why they're so special. Rosemary adds a certain ingredient that will make you feel really good. The ingredient starts with an 'H' and ends with 'ashish.' It wouldn't be right to make you an offer without letting you know."

Jason looked at Youngsoo, unsure of how to react.

"Don't worry, she only adds enough to spice things up a little. Not enough to cause any harm," the lady said.

"Damn straight, we're interested. We're special, too. Just like you," Youngsoo said, taking two brownies, handing one to Jason, as they each bit into the sweet treat.

When the boat cleared the area where the Falls soaked the passengers, the group of seniors removed their ponchos, and the two boys saw that each wore a tee shirt proclaiming themselves as the "Antiquarians."

Laughter erupted. "They are just too much!" Youngsoo said, holding his sides.

"Who came up with that name?' Jason asked a nearby passenger who wore the same shirt.

"See the older lady over there?"

"Uhm, could you be a little more specific?" Jason laughed.

"Of course, that was me being silly," the passenger said. "The one with the rainbow bow in her hair. That's Vivian, the founder of the group. She started singing with a few of the other women in our retirement community. Now, every once in a while, we go out on tour, and we raise money for the local animal shelter. She's a saint, that one."

As if they had rehearsed it and performed the song a hundred times, the entire group of Antiquarians formed a circle around three of their group members, who seemed the be the best singers. Those in the circle began swaying, waving their arms in the air, singing the chorus, "Let the Sunshine In," over and over.

Youngsoo pulled Jason close to him.

"Listen to what they're saying. This song is totally about you. It's dedicated to you. I want to be your sunshine. I want you to let me in. You understand? I want to be in you. You have to let me in. Let your sunshine in. Please do that. It's our destiny," Youngsoo whispered.

During the drive back, Youngsoo told Jason that he was canceling his spa appointment.

"I'll reschedule it and let you know, okay?"

"Sure, okay. No prob."

When Youngsoo pulled into the driveway at Jason's house, Jason sat awkwardly in the passenger seat. He expected something to happen. He wanted something to happen. Disappointment was apparent on his face when Youngsoo simply said, "Ok, see you in class tomorrow."

Though the small amount of the special ingredient added to the brownies was just enough to produce a light buzz, it did heighten Jason's desires, leaving him yearning to "let the sunshine in." He was ready, willing, and able, but Youngsoo said, "Jason, I already said bye for now. I have to get home. Father is expecting me."

Reluctantly, Jason opened the door and stepped out of the car. He felt completely alone, isolated, frustrated, and yet he couldn't deny that this had been one of the best days of his life, though the way the day ended ruined everything.

Chapter Six

B y the time third period Tuesday arrived, the students and staff at Niagara County High were already tired of talking about the bomb scare from the previous day. It was time to move on.

Attendance was at about two-thirds. Some students stayed home in actual fear of possible violence. Others seized the opportunity for one more day free of school, which, to be honest, many of the students found to be hopelessly and endlessly boring.

Mr. Simmons stood at his classroom door, greeting his Honors students as they arrived. He was happy to see all fifteen were present.

"Thanks for your message," he told Jason, squeezing his shoulder as he was about to enter the classroom. "I appreciate what you said. And anytime you want to talk, I'm here for you. Trust me on that."

Jason was all smiles when he entered the room, taking his seat, until he saw Timmy already sitting there, next to Youngmi. He wondered what had happened between the two of them, but it appeared that they were quite cozy, whispering to each other and smiling.

When Jason passed them, on his way to sit next to Young-soo, Youngmi stuck her tongue out at him. "I found out that gay virgins aren't really my type," she sneered, loud enough for everyone to hear. "I found a real killer here, and he's exactly what I've been looking for."

Everyone in class heard the conversation, except for the teacher, who was still in the hallway. The students waited to see how Jason would respond.

Jason, surprised by the verbal attack, said nothing. He secretly hoped that Timmy might come to his defense, but all he did was wrap his arm approvingly around Youngmi's shoulders.

Instead, it was Youngsoo who responded to his sister, saying something in Korean, so no one in the class would know what he said. But her reaction was immediate. She turned away, slinking down in her seat, looking like she was defeated and humiliated. Everyone in the class started talking, commenting, wondering what had just happened.

"You look lovely this morning, my sweetness," Youngsoo said to Jason. "That color is simply perfect for you. Totally fire! And look at that. We match!"

As if no one had noticed that the two boys were wearing matching plum-colored cashmere sweaters. Normally, that would have set the gossip machine into high gear for a week, but the added drama between the two siblings would give the students more than enough to start any number of conspiracy theories going around the school.

"Did you see the reel I posted on Insta about our trip yesterday? It's already in the top five for the day. You're already an influencer. And with me helping with your promos, you're gonna be lit!"

"You didn't post it on TikTok?"

Youngsoo was pleased at the unexpected question from Jason. *So, he is interested in being seen, being admired, getting thousands of likes*, he thought.

"Check for yourself. Wait'll you see the numbers there!" Youngsoo whispered as the teacher entered the room, bringing all chatter from the students to a standstill.

"Welcome back from whatever that was that happened yesterday," Mr. Simmons began. "If you were present for your first two classes this morning, you already heard this, but the administration is requiring every teacher to read this statement at the start of every class today. So here goes."

Mr. Simmons then began reading from a paper in his hand.

"The administration of the Niagara County Public School District has your safety as our highest priority. We want you to know that we will make every effort to ensure that all students are safe whenever they are on our campuses. If you have any information you would like to share about the threat that was received yesterday, you can do so by telling any member of the administration. We assure that your privacy will be protected. Thank you and have a safe and enjoyable day."

"We're also required to ask if anyone would like to comment or express their feelings about what happened. And of course, you may be excused from class to meet with a counselor at any time," Mr. Simmons added.

All the students remained silent as the teacher waited for a full minute.

"Okay. We'll begin today's lesson, then. And please welcome our new student, Youngsoo Kwon, on his first day today."

All eyes were on Youngsoo, who was smiling with delight as he sat next to Jason, in their matching cashmere sweaters.

"You make such a cute couple, kissy, kissy, kissy!" sneered Charles.

This time, Youngmi did not choose to make fun of Charles. Instead, she turned and gave him a thumbs-up, which was the highlight of his day.

"We'll be reading several novels this year, and with each one, I want you to think about these specific aspects of each book we read," Mr. Simmons said, pointing toward the list on the whiteboard.

"One, we always pay attention to the plot. That's basically what happens in the story, the sequence of events, not always told in a linear fashion, of course."

Several hands were raised.

"Let me go through the list first, then we'll have time for questions and comments," he told the class.

"Second, the characters, the people in the story. The author begins with a blank page. Why does the author choose to include certain characters? Are we given a full picture of them? Do you, as a reader, feel a connection to them? And pay attention to the minor characters. Do they provide a different perspective or add important context?"

Mr. Simmons continued going down the list. "Third, the setting, the time and place of the story. How are the characters influenced by the setting? For example, in our first book, *Tess of the D'Urbervilles*, how are the actions of Tess, the main character, determined by the times in which she lived? How do society's attitudes toward women affect the decisions she makes and the actions she takes?"

More hands are raised.

"I know, I'm sure you have many thoughts about this already," the teacher said, glad to have a class with students interested in the course material.

"But let me continue for a bit. Fourth, consider the themes. Does the book include universal themes, such as love, social injustices, or living with grief? What's the underlying message or idea, and of course, there can be several themes included in a novel."

The teacher continued the lesson, wanting to leave questions and discussions for later.

"Fifth, what is the point of view? Is the story being told by a character in the first person? If so, is that person's view restricted to what can actually be seen and heard, or is the character omniscient, able to see and hear everything? Or perhaps, there's an unseen narrator, telling the story in the third person. Be sure to take note of who is telling the story."

Reaching the end of the list, he said, "And finally, what conflicts arise during the narrative? Are they resolved, and if so, how? If not resolved, why not? And if any conflicts are unresolved, how does that make you, as the reader, feel? Does it frustrate you or annoy you? Does it make the story more enjoyable, for you to be left imagining how the story might otherwise end?"

Bringing the lecture to a close, he continued, "Now, of course, this is a lot to think about. But all of it's important, and during this year, we'll dive deeply into each one of these areas."

The next slide on the whiteboard listed the books to be read:

September: *Tess of the D'Urbervilles*, Thomas Hardy, 1891
October: *Lord of the Flies*, William Golding, 1954
November: *The Hate U Give*, Angie Thomas, 2017
December: *If Beale Street Could Talk*, James Baldwin, 1974
January: TBA
February: TBA
Etc.

"Why are we reading *The Birdman of Alcatraz* in January and February?" Susan Malone joked, referring to the TBA.

"Because it's to be determined, TBD, if we'll read *The Bride of Dracula* in March, of course," Tevin replied, trying to outdo his friendly class rival in jokes and puns.

"Is that even a book title?" Susan shot back, as Tevin shrugged, still laughing at his attempt at humor.

"And I know everybody remembers Friday night when I won the game catching that Tess of the D'Urbervilles in the end zone," Tevin added.

Susan gave him a questioning look.

"A TD. A touchdown. Tess of the D'Urbervilles. Get it?"

The entire class, including the teacher, groaned at the awful joke.

"That was a good one, Tevin. Very clever!" Susan said, smiling at her classmate, wanting to get his attention. She was determined to get a boyfriend this school year, and since Timmy didn't show any interest, she wondered whether Tevin would be open to dating a white girl.

Looking him over, she found him to be quite handsome, and there was no doubt that his athletic body was attractive. His mocha skin was flawless, and his brown eyes captivated her. She was thrilled when Tevin smiled back at her.

"Lucky for us, he didn't title it *Saint Tess of the D'Urbervilles*. Then it would be STD," Timmy said, unable to help himself.

"You'll probably have to explain that one to the gay virgin in the back of the room," Youngmi added, nudging her new friend and delighting at least half of the class.

The mood changed immediately when Debi pronounced solemnly, "That list is woke. Are these approved titles for this grade level? As in, approved by the School Board of which my mother is the President?" she demanded to know.

Mr. Simmons sighed. "First, haha to the two clowns, very funny," he said, rolling his eyes in exaggeration. "As all of you well know, TBA means 'to be announced,' and those spaces are left for books that I hope will be suggested by some of you. I want to take your interests into account."

"However," he continued, as Ms. Hampton correctly points out, all titles must be approved by the School Board. And yes, Ms. Hampton, these titles are approved. You can check with your mother, as I'm sure you will anyway."

Debi's arms were folded across her chest in an act of defiance.

"We'll see if these books stay approved after I'm finished speaking to my mother and her friends."

"I'm open to discussing any of the books on the list, and why they were chosen, of course. For example, Baldwin's *If Beale Street Could Talk* is recommended for those 16 years and older. If the class feels you're not mature enough to handle the material, we could substitute something more ... child-friendly."

That comment from the teacher got the entire class talking, debating whether the students in the class, ranging in age from 16 to 17, wanted to be thought of as mature young adults or not.

"I'm not reading anything that my father doesn't personally approve of," shouted Charles. "He makes those decisions for me. No one else."

Another firestorm, as students expressed whether they wanted to make their own decisions or not.

"All right. Calm down, everyone," Mr. Simmons said. "No decisions have to be made today about future books to be read. However, we will begin reading *Tess* today. Does everyone have a copy? I sent the information about class supplies to your parents by email."

Several students shrugged their shoulders, indicating they had no prior knowledge about the need to have purchased the book already.

"Well," the teacher continued. "The School Board, in its wisdom, cut funding for the purchase of books by the school.

They're only paying for certain textbooks, like your Math and Science books. So, you can get your own copy by ordering from ..."

"Can we get the audiobook?" Timmy asked.

"That is an option, but ..."

"Can we just watch the movie?" Debi asked. "I know this book has a movie version."

"Of course, I have no control over whether you watch the movie or not. But let me remind you, this is an Honors English class, meaning that you will read the book, whether you watch the movie or not."

Youngsoo raised his hand.

"Uhm, Mr. Teacher, sorry, I forgot your name, I apologize. But I have a solution for you."

"You do? I'd like to hear it. And my name is Mr. Simmons, for future reference," he said with a smile.

"My father has already purchased a classroom set of the first book for this year. It's his way to make a contribution to the school. He told me that he'll buy class sets of every book we'll read this year. He loves literature, and he wants all of us to be able to enjoy books without worrying about cost."

"Well! That's amazing. And very thoughtful and kind. Please tell your father that I ... I mean, we ... say thank you."

"There should be a delivery in the office for you by now. If you like, I could go check and bring in the box. With your permission, of course, Mr. Simmons."

Youngmi made a sucking noise as Youngsoo left the class, headed for the office.

When he returned, he asked, "Where should I put this?" lifting the already-opened box off the cart. "Of course, it was already opened and searched as a precaution after the bomb scare yesterday," he added.

"Oh, these are perfect!" Mr. Simmons said. "Your father ordered the same edition that I have. It's so much easier when we all have the same edition."

"Of course. Father always does his research. He never makes a mistake."

But Youngsoo wasn't looking at the teacher when he said that. He was looking directly at Jason.

Everyone in the class took a copy from the box, even those who had already purchased their own.

"Let's begin with the content warning," Mr. Simmons said, showing where the passage was located. "It's amazing that Thomas Hardy, way back in 1891, warned readers about this book, which was first published in a serialized version in newspapers. Of course, for its time, it was considered to be quite scandalous, which is why the author decided to include a warning. Listen to what he wrote."

Mr. Simmons read the entire passage, ending with these words:

"... I would ask any too genteel reader who cannot endure to have it said what everybody thinks and feels, to remember a well-worn sentence of St. Jerome's: If an offence come out of the truth, better is it that the offence come than that the truth be concealed."

"And that was written in 1891," Mr. Simmons repeated. "Now, we have content warnings and trigger warnings all the time. In books, in the opening sequences of TV shows, in movies. They're so common that you might just ignore them. But they do serve a purpose.

Today, this book is classified as suitable for ages 13 and up. I tell you that, so no one will be worried about inappropriate content, though I will say that it does deal with some adult situations," he added.

"You'll note that the book is divided into seven phases. The first phase, 'The Maiden' goes from page 7 to 74. The second phase, 'Maiden No More' continues to page 100. I'm going to give you time to begin reading now. Please have the first 100 pages read by the next class on Thursday. Bring with you a short paper, 1 to 2 pages, relating what you've read so far to one of the six aspects of a novel that I showed you earlier. And it's only fair to warn you that I will run all of your papers through an AI checker. You are not permitted to use AI to write any of your assignments for you."

"Dammit!" Debi said, a little too loudly. But several of the students had the exact same thought.

Chapter Seven

"I made reservations for us at the spa this evening. I'll pick you up at six, okay?"

"Can't do. Gotta work tonight."

"No, you don't have to work. We have reservations at the spa. You need to start taking care of your appearance before you start to resemble a wrinkled old prune before the age of 30."

"I'm on the schedule. I'm going in. My mom needs me."

Youngsoo was losing patience.

"Send her a text. Tell her you quit. You don't need that job. You have me now."

Jason pursed his lips stubbornly. "A text? This is my mother we're talking about. She takes care of me, just like she has my entire life. And you want me to disrespect her by quitting my job at her diner by sending a text? That is not going to happen!"

"All right. Let's find a compromise. You can go in and tell her in person that you quit. Then, we'll go right to the spa after that."

"That's your idea of a compromise? You get everything you want, and all I get is your permission to destroy my mother in person instead of by text."

"Well, when you put it like that; I guess that's exactly what I'm saying."

Jason was angry, but he also knew there was some truth to what Youngsoo was saying. It was apparent, even to him, that his life was changing, and tomorrow, during his appointment with Zeus, it might change drastically. And it would be a good idea for him to look his best. Jason knew that Zeus had a keen interest in his looks, though he wasn't sure about his motives yet.

"I'm not quitting. Not tonight. But maybe soon. I'll ask for the night off, and then I'll be free to go to the spa with you. Good enough?"

"I'll be honest. I wish you'd obey me. That would make me very happy. But I see you're still attached to your mother's apron strings ... or her umbilical cord ... so we'll play it your way for now."

"Ok, deal. And please, don't talk about my mom's umbilical cord. Yuck!"

"What's wrong with that? It's part of nature. You do know how babies get made and how they're born, don't you?"

Their laughter eased the tension between them.

Timmy gave Youngmi a ride home in his truck. Before she got out, he leaned in to kiss her, but she turned her face so his lips landed on her cheek.

He felt offended, but said nothing.

I thought Korean girls were supposed to be more obedient than that, he thought, though he had never given a command for her to obey.

Still, he enjoyed watching her go, bouncing into the house. He was thinking about asking her to the first school dance, which was just a few weeks away.

Everyone will know I'm not a virgin if I can be seen at a dance with an actual girl, he thought, still hung up on the idea that others had any thoughts about his virginity. But his classmates had already decided that Timmy must have gone the whole way with some girl during the summer. They had moved on. Timmy, knowing the truth, was still fixated on the subject.

Youngmi waited impatiently in her room for two hours before making the call. She knew she had to wait until 5 PM, or her grandmother in Seoul would be angry at her for calling too early. 5 PM in New York would make it 6 AM the next day in Korea.

"Grandmother, good morning to you. I hope you are well."

Without waiting for an answer, she continued, "May I see him, please?"

Both spoke in Korean, since her grandmother spoke no English at all.

"Yes, granddaughter. He's here. He's a little sleepy. Wait one moment while I go get him."

She returned, holding a 10-month-old baby boy close to the phone's camera.

"You see how beautiful he is. He's growing fast, too. He's going to be a big, strong boy."

Youngmi was in tears.

"Ohhh, my little baby. Look at you, Ji-ho. So handsome. But so fragile and delicate. Before long, you'll grow into the fierce tiger that your name represents. It breaks my heart that I cannot be there with you. Maybe I'll just run away, away from my father, away from America, and go back home and take care of my son."

"Don't even think about it. Father would kill you. And if he doesn't, I'll kill you," came the stern voice of Youngsoo, who had crept up behind her.

"Goodbye, Grandmother. Please be well," Youngsoo said, grabbing the phone from his sister's hand, ending the call.

"Why did you do that? You have no right!"

"I have every right," her brother corrected her. "And you know it's true. I'm the male, and you're the female. You are inferior and subordinate to me. And don't try to argue. We both know the history of our people. If this were the time of the Joseon Dynasty, you would have been killed, or at least left out in the wilderness to die, the day we were born. Fraternal twins were never accepted during Korea's glory days. Only the boy would survive. And you know that I believe in the old ways."

"But the Joseon Dynasty ended in 1897. How long do you intend to believe in the customs of a place that no longer exists?"

"Our culture did not die in 1897. It lives on in me and many others like me. One day, the Dynasty will be restored. That's my vision. I will lead the new Dynasty and I'm going to use ZEUS Universal Group to achieve my goals."

"I hate you," she said.

"Don't be ridiculous. That's like an ant hating the person who's stepping on the entire ant's family without even being aware of their existence. You mean that little to me, so your hatred is a useless emotion. You cannot and you will not hurt me. But I can destroy you," he said, his voice seething with emotion.

As Youngsoo turned to leave, he looked back at his sister and said, "By the way, one more word out of you disrespecting my boyfriend and your new nickname at school will be Tess. You do know the story, right? That she had an illegitimate child, and how she was treated by the men in her life, both before and after she had the baby? Imagine how you'll be treated at school once they find out about your secret past. American teenagers can be vicious, you know."

"Look who's talking," she answered. "Nothing could be worse than the way you treat me."

"You might be surprised," her brother said, as he closed the door behind him, leaving her to sob in loneliness and despair. "I can make things a million times worse for you."

Youngsoo waited in the car while Jason went into the diner to see his mother.

"Hey, you have a new poster in the window. I didn't know the Antiquarians were performing in town. I saw them on the Maid of the Mist tour. They were pretty awesome."

"You saw them on the Maid of the Mist? When was that?"

"Monday, the day we had off from school. They were on the same boat as us. They sang a great song about the sunshine."

"Yes, I know the song. Some members of the group were in for lunch today, and they asked if they could put the sign in the window. They want everybody in town to know that tickets are available for their show."

"You should go see them. I think you'd have fun. And maybe you could ask someone to go with you. Maybe you have your eye on some man, I don't know. Because I'm not gonna be your little boy for you to take care of forever. You know that, right?"

"Of course, I know you're growing up, Cupcake. But you'll always be my little boy. That doesn't change for a mother. And don't be in too much of a rush. You're still in high school, you know."

Even though she said the words, she knew it was wishful thinking. Sooner or later, she'd have to face the fact that Jason would have his own life to live, making choices that perhaps she wouldn't approve of.

"One lady from the group said the funniest thing. They ordered the brownies for dessert, and you know I pride myself on having the best brownies in Niagara County. But she said that there seemed to be something missing in them. Do you think she wanted walnuts? Should I add them?"

"No, Mom. I don't know what she thought, but I do know the regulars here would be mighty upset if you changed the recipe."

Jason was giggling on the inside, knowing that he'd never be able to explain how he knew that the missing ingredient started with an "H" and ended with "ashish."

"Tell me more about your trip to the Falls. Was it romantic? Which girl did you take? Someone new?"

"No, no girl."

A look of confusion came over his mother's face.

"Are you trying to tell me something? Did you go with a boy? Should I sit down here and prepare myself for the shock of my life?"

She continued to speak, changing the subject, reminiscing about the last time she went on a tour of the Falls. Jason chose not to respond to her question about being with a boy.

"You know, Cupcake, your father took me on the Maid of the Mist. It was our honeymoon, and it was such a beautiful night that we spent together. We stayed in one of the fancy hotels, you know, the ones with the heart-shaped beds. And nine months later, you were born."

"Oh, Mom, don't tell me stuff like that."

"Why not, sweetie? What your dad and I did that night was a beautiful thing. That's how two people show their love for each other. It's perfectly natural, and there's nothing wrong with it. And look at what came out of our love — the most beautiful boy in the world."

"You're right, it's natural. But no kid wants to think about what their parents did. Ugh!"

Katrina sighed, already thinking about the beautiful grand-babies that Jason would produce someday, creating the next generation and passing along the family legacy.

"One night, you'll take your bride to one of the honeymoon hotels and ..."

"Stop it, Mom. We'll talk about it later. Right now, I want to know if I can get the night off. It's important."

Katrina looked out at the parking lot, noticing the red sports car waiting there.

"Cupcake, you're worrying me. Is everything okay? Are you in some kind of trouble?"

"Mom, listen, I'd love to tell you the whole story, but I can't right now. I have to go. I promise I'll make up the shift later this week. Can you just get someone to cover me for tonight?"

Jason didn't wait for an answer. He was worried that if they talked anymore at that moment, his mother would learn too much, too soon. He wasn't ready to tell her everything yet.

Youngsoo was waiting in the car, with two nervous Frenchies peering out the passenger window, who were wondering when Jason would reappear, with doggie treats in hand. They knew a trip to the diner meant that pup cups would soon be served.

It had been Youngsoo's idea to include them on the trip tonight.

"Bring the girls along!" he said, when Jason had greeted him at his front door just a little earlier. "They can have a girls' night, while we enjoy our boys' night."

"But ..."

"Why do you always resist? Lighten up. Let's have fun. You know they love to be pampered."

Jason couldn't argue with that. Smiley Myrus and Polly Darton were spoiled, and Jason wouldn't have it any other way. They were his babies.

After Jason joined the trio back in the car, they headed straight for the pet shop.

"Give them the full treatment," Youngsoo instructed the groomers. "Nails, ears, bath, even a massage. Make them feel like they're living in luxury."

"And I see you have some cute little outfits over there. Dress them up for us. My girls just love to get dressed up and dolled up." Jason added.

"That's the spirit. Splurge a little. Have fun. Spend money. We have it, so we're gonna flaunt it," Youngsoo said, grinning as he saw the changes in Jason's attitude.

The groomers were happy to oblige because working with animals, especially two adorable Frenchies, was what they enjoyed.

"We'll be back in two hours, OK?" Jason asked, before heading for the door.

"Make that three," Youngsoo called back to the groomers. "We have a lot to do and I don't ever like to be late."

Jason wasn't sure how to act at the spa, so he decided to follow Youngsoo's lead. Although he'd only been in town for a few days, it was clear that this wasn't his first trip to this particular spa, as he was greeted warmly by the hostess.

"Rule Number One," he told Jason, "is to relax. No outside thoughts, no intrusions, just pure enjoyment of the moment. Experience and savor every sensation. For me, this is pure pleasure."

Jason did his best to follow that advice, to clear his mind of any disturbing thoughts. He felt like he was floating during the facial, in a state of total relaxation.

While the manicures and pedicures were being done, he gave in to the urge to discuss his feelings, as he experienced a tightening bond with his new friend.

"I feel like I've been looking at life with blinders on, only seeing a small part of what's in front of me. Now, I can see many more possibilities, and many more ways of thinking."

Youngsoo replied, "A man wearing blinders should expect to be blind-sided."

Yes, exactly that! Jason thought. *I have to be open to new opportunities.*

The two boys, each wearing only the luxuriously soft bathrobes they were given at the start of the session, smiled at each other. Jason couldn't help but admire the strong legs of the young man next to him, watching as his feet were being massaged, wishing that perhaps he might one day do the same thing — or perhaps have Youngsoo at his feet, massaging away the cares of the outside world.

"I'll take the clear polish," Youngsoo told the manicurist. "I prefer to present myself as masculine, but well-groomed. But I don't know what Jason wants. Maybe pink? I think you're a bit more effeminate than I am."

Jason smiled, but told his manicurist, "I also want the clear polish. But, let me see how it looks with a very light pink color, but only on my pinkies. That might be cute."

"Good choice for you. I agree. Let's see how it looks," Youngsoo agreed.

As the manicurists followed their orders, Youngsoo said to Jason, "I have a secret to share with you. Tomorrow, Zeus is going to make you an offer. He's very excited to have you become part of his companies. I heard Father talking about it. I couldn't hear everything he said, but I did hear the words 'long-term contract' and 'possibly in the millions.' This is why it's very important for you to be open-minded. If you answer them correctly, your life can change in an instant."

"What do they want from me? Do you know?"

"They want your face to be the face of a new product line. But you will have to make sacrifices. Success doesn't come without costs. I think you already know that, but the price, well, maybe the price will be too high. That's the decision you'll have to make."

Jason couldn't imagine what Zeus might ask of him that would be too high a price. He decided not to ask. Better to find out the terms from the only true source: Zeus himself.

"It's time for your massages. Please follow me to the back room. We always want to assure privacy for our clients," the hostess told them.

"We want to get our massages in the same room," Youngsoo said.

"Are you sure?"

"Yes!" Youngsoo snapped at her. "Do not make me repeat myself."

Jason was surprised at how Youngsoo treated these women, though he should have expected it.

The two boys were led into a large room, with two massage tables in the center.

"Turn around and face the wall, Jason."

Without thinking, Jason obeyed. Whenever Youngsoo gave him some type of order, Jason always thought about Timmy. It had never been like that with him. They were best friends and equal partners. But this, whatever this was with Youngsoo, felt very different.

The boys in Love, Simon didn't act that way, Jason thought. So he knew it wasn't necessary for one of the boys to be "in charge," though he also couldn't claim that he minded it.

"I don't want my boyfriend to see me in this state of arousal. If he sees me this way, he'll know how much I want him," Youngsoo told his masseuse, teasingly, easing himself onto the table, face down.

"Jason, you may get on your table now."

The young ladies began working on the muscular bodies of the two teens, each of them relaxing under the strong hands of the young women.

"These bitches do a pretty good job, don't you think?" Youngsoo asked.

"Don't call them bitches. Treat them with respect. Why do you talk like that? And right in front of them. It isn't right."

Looking up at his masseuse, Jason said, "Don't listen to Mr. Misogyny over there. He isn't used to American women and their freedoms. Not yet, anyway."

Youngsoo laughed. "Have you even seen who is working on you? These girls aren't American. They're from Korea. Same as me. They know the Korean ways. They want to serve strong men, which is what they're doing right now."

"And by the way, I love that name you just gave me. Mr. Misogyny. It suits me very well. Ladies, when I come in here, I want you to always refer to me as Mr. Misogyny."

Everyone in the room laughed at that, though for different reasons.

Turning over to lie on his back, Youngsoo continued, "If Zeus keeps my father in this backwater town for any length of time, I'll have to have some young men brought in to do my massages. The women do a nice job, but there's nothing quite as fine as having a man with a muscular body and a submissive attitude massaging me, following my directions in an obedient manner."

"Wait. You might not be here for very long?" Jason suddenly grew concerned. He was beginning to think about Youngsoo in the long-term.

"The same is true for you," Youngsoo replied. "But Zeus will discuss that with you. My hope is that my father will return to Greece, to the international headquarters of the company, when Zeus goes back. There's no way Zeus would ever take up permanent residence here. He's much too sophisticated and cosmopolitan to live here in Hickstown."

Those words stopped Jason. It made sense. Of course, this had to be a temporary arrangement for Zeus.

"And those Greek men ... so very sexy!" Youngsoo sighed. "I want to go to Athens and be among the ancient Greek gods. Though we have our own Korean mythologies, I find the stories of the ancient Greeks to be fascinating!" he gushed.

"Would Sir enjoy a happy ending?" the masseuse working on Youngsoo asked, interrupting his conversation.

"When you phrase it like that, of course, Sir would *enjoy* a happy ending. But I will not require one tonight. And if my boyfriend over there wants one, he is not allowed to have one. Understand?"

"Wait a minute. Hold on. What if I say I want one? Don't I get to make that decision?"

"Who's paying?" the masseuse asked.

Youngsoo raised his hand, waving it in the air.

"Then no happy ending for you!" she said, laughing and pointing at Jason.

Jason dropped the conversation. He had so much to think about. First, the possibility, no, the probability that Youngsoo would not be staying in Niagara for very long. Second, it seemed that Youngsoo already had a "happy ending," probably in that very room, with one of these females.

What does that mean? Is he bi? Am I prepared to get involved in a relationship with someone for whom sex is so casual? And if Youngsoo did it with one of these girls, why hasn't he done it with me, yet? he wondered. But one thought eased his concerns. *That's twice already that he called me his boyfriend. It's finally happening!*

On the way to pick up Jason's two bestest girls, Smiley and Polly, Youngsoo said, "I know you didn't really want a happy ending at the spa, especially not from a female."

Jason sat quietly, listening.

"But maybe I can interest you in something that I think is a better deal — a happily-ever-after," Youngsoo continued, hoping that Jason was thinking along the same lines.

"No, they only exist in fairy tales and romance novels!" Jason replied, only half-jokingly.

Youngsoo was disappointed by that response. "I disagree. I think it's possible in real life for two people to live happily ever after. That's one of my goals in this lifetime. I hope you'll be there with me."

Jason's heart was leaping with joy, but he showed no emotion. This was exactly what he had always dreamed of, and now it was happening, and yet, he wasn't quite ready to make the leap into Youngsoo's life completely.

Before they could continue talking, they reached their destination. Youngsoo decided to let the topic go, but just for the moment.

"They look so adorable!" Jason shouted when he saw his two little furries, waiting impatiently for their Daddy to take them home.

"They really are!" Youngsoo agreed, eyeing their cute skirts, with coordinating hats and matching sunglasses. He instantly started taking photos, never missing an opportunity to get images for social media posts.

Jason carried one in each arm as they headed for the car and the short ride back to Jason's house. Once there, the two girls ran up to the porch, ready to go inside and have their dinner served. They knew they had trained Jason well, and Jason wouldn't argue if anyone ever called them spoiled.

"Do you like me?" Youngsoo asked, before Jason could get out of the car..

"Yes, very much," Jason said, without hesitation, settling back into his seat, ready to talk.

"I know I have some old-fashioned ways. But I want you to understand that I come from an ancient culture. Many things have changed in Korea, but I long for the old ways, the days of the Joseon Dynasty, which lasted from 1392 to 1897. One day, I would like to lead my nation, just like the Emperor Taejo of Joeson did. I would impose my vision on my countrymen and have them serve me as their god. That's why I need the riches of Zeus. That's why I'm going to replace him. This is my plan. If you understand this, then you understand me."

"I never knew anyone who wanted to be an emperor-god before. Would it surprise you if I said I need some time to process this?"

"I understand. But there's more. Just like I believe that I'm a god, the reincarnation of Taejo, I also believe that you're a god. You, however, are one of the ancient Greek gods. I'm sure of it. I think Zeus recognizes that in you. Perhaps he fears you and wants to control you. If we join forces, who knows what the future will hold for us? An empire combining Asia and Europe, with the two of us as the god-heads. Just imagine the power we might have!"

"You dream big. I never thought of anything even close to that before, especially for my own future. But I heard what you said about not wearing blinders and I think you're right. At the very least, I need to expand my thinking about what's possible for me."

Jason continued speaking. "But I have to ask, do you even like me? I heard what you said about being aroused, but maybe you were just teasing me. I don't know, since I wasn't allowed to look. And if you do like me, then why haven't we ...?"

"Stop right there," Youngsoo told him. "I was aroused at the spa. I'm aroused right now, to the point of physical pain. I want you so badly that I could scream."

"Then why not?"

"It's simple. I want our first time to be a fabulous, mystical, incredible experience. One we'll never forget. So, I didn't want a quickie in a cave, or a minuteman special in the car. That's why I'm asking you right now to be my date for the school dance. It's in two weeks. I want us to make it officially known at the dance that we're a couple, and we'll be the most fabulously dressed guys there. I want us to be the center of attention. And then, after the dance, I'll take you to a luxurious hotel suite, with a view of the Falls, and that night, we will be joined together. I know that we're destined for a future together. That night will be the first of many, many physical encounters. After that night, you'll belong completely to me."

"So, Jason, my Greek god, will you be my date for the school dance?"

"You don't know how much I've wanted to hear those words from you. Of course, I'll be your date, and we'll be together in front of all our classmates and teachers; everyone will see us. I'm so excited!"

Once inside the house, after feeding Smiley and Polly, Jason went into his bedroom, removed all of his clothes and stood, staring at his image in the full-length mirror on his closet door.

He knew he was handsome, but he was also plagued with doubts. Despite his best efforts at exuding an air of confidence, he often considered himself unworthy of any attention at all.

He started to think that everything Youngsoo had said about the future was absurd.

Talk of ancient gods, emperors, where did all that come from? I'm just a kid living in a small town in New York State. I'm not a Greek god. That's ridiculous.

And look at me. I look like a clown, he continued to think, going back to his usual habits of self-doubt and worry.

What will Mom think if she sees me in nail polish? What about this pink lipstick? Why did I let Youngsoo talk me into this?

"What am I doing?" he shouted at his image.

He went into his mother's bathroom and found her nail polish remover, scrubbing his nails clean. He used her makeup remover to hide any trace of lipstick, eye shadow, or mascara.

I must be crazy to think I can act this way, here in Niagara Falls, and get away with it, he was thinking, having a vision of the entire school football team attacking him, beating him senseless.

I can hide myself. I can blend in. I don't have to be a peacock flaunting my tail feathers in the wind for all to see.

Crying, in a state of confusion, he covered himself completely in his bed, hiding from the world, wishing that someone would give him some simple answers about how life is supposed to be.

Why couldn't my plans for a simple, quiet life with Timmy come true? With that thought, he fell asleep.

Chapter Eight

I t's a typical Friday at Niagara County High School, with cheerleaders prancing the halls in their cute uniforms, teasing the boys, and generating "school spirit" for the pep rally later that afternoon and the big football game that evening.

Charles Bannon, awkwardly carrying an armful of books in his skinny arms, accidentally bumped into one of the cutest girls, one of the most popular girls, knocking her one notebook to the floor.

"Don't touch me, you ugly creep! Crawl back into your hole with the rest of the monsters."

Then, turning to one of her fellow cheerleaders, she said, "Can you believe they let them walk out here in the sunlight? They should be hidden away unless, by some miracle, a doctor could make them even look human."

Before the girls could skip away, Charles, who would normally slink off without a word, decided that he'd had enough.

"Has it ever occurred to you that if someone doesn't meet your standards of beauty, that maybe they've already been informed of that fact, like a million times already, and maybe they're all too aware of the fact and maybe, just maybe, they really don't feel like hearing about it again?"

His face was red with anger as he shouted his feelings.

"Oh, look, it has thoughts," the girl said, turning her back and walking away, waving back at him dismissively.

This being a high school in the 21st Century, the incident was, of course, caught on video by several students, and seconds later, the scene was shared on social media.

Comments were posted just as quickly.

"Hey bud, if you start a GoFundMe for some paper bags to cover your ugly mug, I'll be the first to contribute."

"The nerve of him to bump into her like that. She should file an assault charge."

"Dude, you actually go outside? Yikes!"

"Look at Mr. String Bean trying to violate the space of the cool kids. Got what he deserved."

"The loser nerd has the hots for the girlie. He'll never get her. Why did he even try?"

"I wish you a long, miserable life as an incel. Get used to it, cause you ain't never gonna get any."

Hundreds and hundreds of comments. Not one mentioned how the cheerleader talked to her fellow student.

Charles, and everyone else at school, knew the outcome beforehand. The world doesn't like ugly people and the world will provide plenty of excuses for those deemed attractive. Charles is expected to accept his fate, as already determined by others. He's supposed to accept being defeated in life. Inside, he's a volcano about to erupt, but he tries to hide it.

He had no one to talk to, until he found some chat rooms where he felt welcomed, valued, and he could share his stories with those who were being treated just like the world treats him. Talk of revenge fills the conversations there.

Youngmi spent the day feeling like every set of eyes was on her. She was convinced that her brother had already told everyone about her baby, left back in Korea.

She imagined what they were whispering behind her back.

"She abandoned her baby. What kind of mother does that?

"What a slut. That's how Asian girls are. Loosey-goosey."

"I knew it the minute I saw her. No morals. No decency. Clearly, not raised with good Christian moral values."

Throughout the day, she avoided making direct eye contact with anyone, despite the fact that her brother hadn't said a word to anyone. Not even his boyfriend.

He had threatened to expose his sister's past, and he would if he felt it became necessary to put her in her place, but Youngsoo was consumed with thoughts of his own power. Joining forces with Jason and achieving greatness together was an exciting prospect. Besides that, he was also looking forward to taking his boyfriend to the school dance and later spending a night of pleasure together.

Timmy had spent all of Thursday night working on an assignment for his elective Creative Writing class. The teacher told the class to write a short piece, in any style, exploring the power of repetition.

Or, as the teacher had phrased it, "The power of repetition, repetition, repetition."

He was the first to volunteer to read his work aloud in class.

Eggs crack, bros chirp
My world of hunger and cold

The warmth of Mama
Shields me from the biting winds
I am Eagle

Father strong
In regal flight
I watch to learn
I must survive
I am Eagle

Solo flights
Days and nights
I search for prey and
For my mate, to procreate
I am Eagle

The arrow strikes
My spirit flies
Limp body falls
Failure is mine
I am Eagle

I should have soared
And ruled the skies
Life wasn't fair
All alone I died
I am Eagle

Timmy cared little about the teacher's comments, which went unheard by Timmy. He'd written the piece thinking about the day that he and Jason had gone fishing. Their last day as best friends. For Timmy, the words were about his longing for Jason.

He wanted to send a copy to Jason, but he wasn't sure if he should. That's all he thought about for the rest of the day. Send it, or not?

At the end of the school day, Timmy decided that it couldn't hurt. Maybe Jason wouldn't even open the message. But if he did, he hoped that Jason would also remember the time they spent together and maybe understand that Timmy was sorry about what he had done.

Jason spent the day doing his best to avoid Youngsoo.

"There you are!" he said, sliding into the seat next to Jason at lunch.

"Look at your hands. So plain. Is that how you want to present yourself to Zeus this afternoon?"

"Oh, I scratched one nail, and then the rest of them didn't look right, so I decided it would be better if they all matched. And I can't paint them myself, so I just took it all off."

"Ok, if that's what you want me to think," Youngsoo replied, knowing that Jason was lying. "You're still beautiful. Zeus might still offer you the position."

Youngsoo was well aware that a little nail polish and make-up, or lack thereof, would make no difference to Zeus, who already knew whom he wanted. But Youngsoo wanted to be able to claim some of the credit for Jason's success, and now that effort had been lost.

"I guess I'll just have to accomplish it on my own," Jason answered, unaware of how closely he had nailed the situation.

After school, Jason headed home to prepare for his meeting with Zeus. Entering the house, he saw that his mother had left a note and a small package.

Cupcake,

Your father left this for you, with instructions for you to open it on your 18th birthday. I think you might need to hear from him now. I know changes are coming very quickly. Please listen to your father. It's better that the two of you have time alone, so I went into work early.

Mom

Jason sat at the dining table, on a sturdy, reupholstered seat, with his elbows leaning on the table, then reached gently for the manila envelope. Taking a deep breath, he pulled it open and held the letter with trembling hands.

Son,

I hope you never read this. I'm headed off to fight in a war that I don't understand. I hope it's a just war. If I die, I want it to be for a just cause. But the honest truth is, I don't know.

I'm a man of honor. My country has called me. Doing my duty is important to me.

If I don't return, I want you to read this as you are becoming a man — on your 18th birthday.

Do you know why your name is Jason Masters? When I saw you on the day you were born, already blonde, with a full head of hair, I had one thought. The Golden Fleece. I hope you know the story from our Greek heritage. The fleece is a symbol of power. For a baby to be born, already golden, revealed to me that you are a powerful one. Use your power wisely, my son.

Your name is a symbol of that power. But sometimes, the name isn't the most important part of a man's heritage.

Why do I mention this? It's because I changed my name. Not to hide. Not to change the nature of my being. I did it as a way to show that I was ready to leave the old ways behind, to face new adventures in new surroundings.

I hope the name I chose for you is a reflection of your true self. But how can I know that? You alone can decide whether my choice is suitable or not.

I want you to find the true meaning of your life and live it to the fullest. Do you know that my soul is a part of you? We have an unbreakable bond. That of Father and Son. No one can take that from us.

Now that you are approaching maturity, make good decisions. Not just for yourself, but for your family, as well. No one flies solo in the world.

Spread your wings. Live fearlessly. Show your courage. If not, a life filled with regrets awaits you.

Allow me to offer these words of advice. Find something that you treasure, like Jason and the Argonauts sought after the Golden Fleece, believing that it would allow Jason to become his true self: a King.

But do not limit your search to physical things. Even more importantly, find a person you can treasure. Whether others approve or not, use your power to protect and honor the one you love. There can be no greater honor in life than finding someone to treasure and who feels the same about you.

Finally, honor and protect your mother for as long as she lives. Katrina is my treasure. I love you both.

I want you to always remember and honor my name.

I am Giorgios Mastrogogiannis. I am George Masters.

I left something for you in the box. It's one of my treasures—our family shield. It was handed down from my great-grandfather to my grandfather, then to my father, who gave it to me. Now, it is yours. I hope you will treasure it and pass it along to the next generation.

Papa

Jason was stunned. It was almost too much to take in. Despite having no real memories of his father, it seemed that his dad knew him very well. *How could he possibly know my current situation and give me such good advice?* he wondered.

Jason didn't remember ever calling his father "Papa," but he assumed that must have been his childhood name for him.

And his comments about the Golden Fleece, the advice to seek his treasure, his wisdom about changing names. Jason had so much to think about.

He stared at the small box for a moment, then opened it gently, seeing his family crest for the first time. In the middle, a golden "M" for Mastrogogiannis, a Greek name for Master. Surrounding it, an image of an eagle, the symbol for Zeus, clutching several arrows, an olive wreath, such as those worn by Greek nobility, and a thunderbolt, looking much like the one dangling from the chain around Jason's neck.

Seeing that reminded Jason of Zeus's words to him:

"We need a fresh, young face. We will decide soon if he will be named as our Ganymede."

Just then, Jason had a revelation. He went over to grab a piece of paper out of his mother's printer. Going back to the dining table, he took a marker and wrote, in bold letters:

Giorgios **M**astrogogiannis

George **M**asters

Gany **M**ede

He felt as if he had solved a riddle, left for him many years ago by the man he now thought of as Papa.

It is okay for me to change my name. It is okay for me to become Ganymede. This was my destiny all along!

His confidence in making the decision was strong, and he was eager to meet with Zeus.

Waiting in the anteroom outside of Zeus's office, Jason was surprised to find a message on his phone from Timmy. When he read Timmy's words, these lines struck him the most:

Solo flights
Days and nights
I search for prey
For my mate, to procreate
I am Eagle
Do straight guys always have to be so focused on reproducing? What's wrong with just loving someone, without having a need to pass on your DNA? he thought.

Timmy would have answered that he was trying to poetically describe the life cycle of an eagle, while also making a point about the fragility of life and missing out on opportunities. But Jason didn't send a reply asking Timmy what he meant, so of course, Timmy couldn't defend his piece.

"Mr. Vasiliadis will see you now. Please follow me."

Jason followed the receptionist into the expansive boardroom of this small satellite office of ZEUS Universal to find Zeus seated at the head of a long conference table.

"Hello, my darling boy! Thank you for agreeing to meet with me. How are you? And how's your mother?"

"We're both fine, Sir. Thanks for asking. What a beautiful room this is!"

"This is nothing. You should see our headquarters in Athens. I built that place to impress. You know, when I invite my fellow billionaires over so we can discuss how we'll take over the world."

"Ohhh," Jason replied, with a worried look on his face.

Zeus walked over to where Jason was standing, taking him by the hand and leading him to the chair next to his.

"Do you always take everyone so seriously? That was my attempt at a joke. Do you think I have to work on my delivery?"

"No, Sir. I mean, I don't know you well enough to know if you're joking. And I might add, this is all a little intimidating for me."

"Of course it is," Zeus replied. "I do understand. I want you to become completely comfortable in my presence, where you'll feel at ease telling me anything and everything. I also want you to become comfortable with a different lifestyle. That's why you're here. I want to offer you a life of decadent luxury. Would you like that?"

"Yes, I believe I would," Jason answered, smiling.

"Normally, I'd have one of my associates make a presentation to you about the offer. But you ... you're very different, very special. I've taken a personal interest in you. A deeply personal interest."

"Please, go on. I'm dying to hear what you have to say."

"First, let me give you the vision. I've had my scientists working on new formulas for men's beauty and grooming products. Completely natural ingredients, all proven to be effective against common problems such as aging skin, thinning hair, even belly fat."

Jason laughed, trying to imagine himself with any belly fat at all, but unable to conjure the image.

"Think of all the ads you see constantly for women's beauty products. We're going to saturate the markets with ads for these men's products, all under the umbrella title of IMMORTAL. This market is potentially worth billions, and I want you to be the face associated with the brand."

"Where do I sign?" Jason asked, only half-jokingly.

"I appreciate your enthusiasm. It's an exciting project, and I'm looking forward to its launch in just a few weeks. But there's a lot to be done before then."

"Such as?"

"Today, I want to go over the contract terms with you. It will be a lifetime contract, meaning you can never do any modeling work for any companies other than my own."

"So far, I don't see any problems."

"Lifetime. That means for your entire life. I want a total commitment from you, or the deal will never happen."

Zeus continued, saying, "You will change your name to Ganymede. That's how you'll be introduced and presented to the public. It's a very special name with a very special meaning."

"Yes, I know. One of the moons of Jupiter."

Zeus looked at Jason questioningly, but continued speaking.

"I will take you to live with me in Athens. This is a must. I need you in close proximity to me. You'll be one of my most valuable assets — a treasure, actually, and I need to keep a close eye on you."

"But what about my mother? Can she come along?"

"Ganymede, listen. You have to cut your past ties. This is your future we're talking about. Not your mother's."

Seeing Jason's disappointment, Zeus said, "Of course, you can talk to her anytime you want. Just use your phone."

"And, as an added bonus, I'll be bringing Hades back to Athens with me, too."

"Hades?" Jason asked.

"You know him as Mr. Kwon. Of course, he'll bring his children with him to live in Greece as well. I believe you have an interest in his son. Isn't he your boyfriend? I would hope you'd enjoy having him with you, and the two of you will be stunning additions to the gay culture in my city," Zeus said, positively beaming at the thought.

Jason shifted uneasily in his chair. He wasn't used to speaking openly about his relationship with Youngsoo. Not yet.

"I want to start the process today, with my photographers taking a series of promotional shots of you. I have people ready right now to assist you with wardrobe, hair, makeup, and whatever else needs to be done. But first, I need you to sign these documents, including an NDA."

"An NBA?" Jason asked, confused.

"Oh, my dear boy! You are too cute sometimes. No, a non-disclosure agreement. That means you can never reveal anything about our operations at ZEUS Universal. You may not reveal your salary, or any conditions set on you for being paid, or anything about the secret formulas used in the products. It's standard in this business."

"Salary? We haven't talked about that, yet."

"Good point. After you sign these documents, $250,000 will be deposited into your bank account. You'll see the transaction first thing in the morning. I'm doing this in advance to show my trust in you, because the documents won't be legally binding until your mother also signs them, since you're underage. I'm sure you can convince her to sign."

"I know she wants what's best for me. I think she'll agree to the terms."

"Oh," Zeus said, "one more important point. If you violate the terms of the contract, including the NDA, then you'll immediately lose everything. Right now, that might not seem important, but you'll feel differently when you'll have millions and millions of dollars to lose."

"I understand. I'm ready to sign."

"Good. But there's one more thing before that. I want to see the entire product that I'm purchasing. Stand up and take off all your clothes. I have to be aware of any imperfections, and this is the only way I can be sure. It's okay to have a few things wrong or maybe out of proportion, but I have to be aware so those things can be fixed."

He thinks of me as a product, not a person. Am I okay with that? Jason wondered, but that thought didn't prevent him from removing his clothing and allowing Zeus to inspect him thoroughly. Jason was somewhat surprised that throughout the process, Zeus never laid a finger on him.

"How is it that the gods created such a perfect specimen when they made you?" Zeus asked rhetorically. "I've never seen anyone like you. Zero imperfections. If I didn't know better, I'd say that you were designed by the gods specifically to be immortal, a deity for all mortals to aspire to."

"If I were to make one suggestion, it might be that your nails would look better with some polish. Being properly groomed while in the public eye is essential," Zeus said, winking.

Jason had to wonder if somehow Youngsoo had managed to contact Zeus about him removing his nail polish.

That's a silly thought!

Or was it? Is everyone at ZEUS Universal so connected that they share everything that happens?

Sitting down, Zeus told his Ganymede to leave his clothing and to wear the robe that was neatly folded on the seat next to Jason's.

"The designers will dress you for the photo shoots. No need to wear those things," Zeus said.

"You passed my inspection 100%. I'm ready to go forward with the contract. Do you have any questions before you sign?"

"Should I sign my old name or sign as Ganymede?"

"Oh, I do like your style! We're going to get along fabulously. And of course, sign with your legal name."

Jason did as he was asked.

"Off you go, then," Zeus said. "My assistants will take over from here. But let me assure you, Ganymede, you will never regret this day. It's a good time to be alive, rich, and famous!"

With that, Zeus left the room, and the receptionist entered to escort him to the area where the photoshoot would take place.

It was like a dream experience for Jason. Having his makeup done by professionals, his hair teased to look tousled to perfection, his clothing selected for him by designers. All attention on him. He decided that he could easily get used to this life. In fact, he was convincing himself that this was always his goal, though in reality he had no such dreams before meeting Zeus.

In the course of a few hours, thousands of photos had been taken. The best would be used for the product promotions, as determined by Zeus's editorial staff.

"There'll be one more set," the photographer told him. "Zeus uses a special photographer for the more intimate photos. He'll be taking over. Please remove all clothing and go through that door. The room will be dark, but your eyes will grow accustomed to it, eventually."

More intimate photos? Remove all my clothing?

Jason was unprepared for this development. Still, the thought of earning $250,000 for a few hours of modeling overcame his inhibitions. He obeyed willingly.

Jason entered a room devoid of any light source. Walking blindly forward, using care not to trip or fall, he found himself on some sort of stage.

Behind him, a door opened, and he turned to see a figure in dark clothing approaching him. He only had a glance, but it appeared that the photographer was wearing a bodysuit, with a cloak swirling about him, and some sort of mask.

His first thought was something along the lines of:

Isn't this the part of the horror movie where the audience thinks that the character should have seen this coming?

The photographer spoke in a voice that sounded robotic, making Jason think that the mask had some sort of audio device to change the man's voice. The brief glimpse of the skin-tight bodysuit had confirmed that the photographer was a man. No doubt about that.

There were no introductions, no chit-chat to put Jason at ease, like during the earlier sessions.

"There will be three portions of this session. Follow my directions exactly. Move over there," the photographer said, pointing to an area that was suddenly flooded with lights.

Jason walked over to a set that had a chair, a bed, and a bathtub filled with water.

"The first session is titled 'Supple,' and in order to achieve that, think of yourself as a liquid. But don't take that literally, as in, don't use the water in the tub as you might in real life. Make your body become liquid. Move as if you are liquid. Think of how liquid spreads, how it takes the shape of a container, how it can be poured onto or into something. Move in that way and I'll capture your essence on film as you move."

Jason began moving stiffly, unsure what to do.

"No, not like that! Is that your body being liquid? Do you think of liquid as a stiff form? Be loose! Be free! Don't pose. Just move, as liquid would. You are a beautiful river, then you transform into a peaceful lake, and then you become the roaring Falls of Niagara. Do it!"

Jason began moving gracefully, as if he had indeed become liquid.

"Yes! Yes! That's it. You are so beautiful and you're a natural at modeling. This is exactly how I pictured you!" came the flat, robotic voice.

Jason used the props to full effect, draping himself at times over them, taking their shape, spreading himself over them.

"Excellent! Now, take a moment to transform from the supple state into the next phase, titled 'Rigid.' I want you to return to the stiff movements you were using at the beginning, thinking of yourself as a piece of wood. Use angles, use twists like you might see in a tree, but keep your movements as stiff as you possibly can. Begin to move and I'll capture you at the best angles."

Jason did as instructed while the photographer captured each movement.

"Every part of your body could become stiff. Do you under-stand me?"

"You want me to ...?"

"I want nothing from you. Do what comes naturally. The title of this segment is 'Rigid.' Your job is to be rigid. Am I clear enough?"

Being photographed by a mysterious stranger, with an el-ement of possible danger, was enough to ignite Jason's imag-ination, achieving the rigidity and stiffness that was required during this part of the assignment.

Jason accepted that this was a job requirement. He wasn't about to let any false modesty stand in the way of his future as a supermodel and spokesman for IMMORTAL.

"Ohhh, that is perfect!" came the robot voice.

Occasionally, the flash from the camera would allow Jason to get a glimpse of the photographer, who had removed his cloak, now clad only in the black bodysuit and the epee mask, the type worn by people engaged in the sport of fencing.

For the most part, Jason ignored the presence of the photographer, who was skilled at placing his subjects in a state of mind that was other-worldly.

"Section Three — The Beast," he announced. "Neither liquid nor wooden, during this phase I want to capture your animalistic nature. Begin with your aggressive masculinity. Act as men do when they are behaving badly. Then, transform to show your submissive, effeminate side. Do not be shy. Do not be afraid. Unleash the beast within. These photos will be the cream on top. Show me all of your hidden desires, your secrets, expose yourself for all the world to see!"

Jason, feeling completely free and unrestrained, posed in ways that he had never imagined before. Starkly intimate, displaying emotions from rage to total calm, from screaming to silence, from eruption to implosion, from penetrator to becoming the object being penetrated.

As Jason reached the point of exhaustion, feeling as though he had nothing left to give, the room once more went black. A door opened, and Jason watched as the photographer left, without a word of thanks or goodbye, leaving Jason alone.

He looked around, but his clothes seemed to be gone.

Of course, I undressed before I came in here, he thought.

He found his way to the door, but it wouldn't open. In a sudden panic, thinking perhaps he was indeed trapped in a horror movie, he pounded on the door frantically.

"Sorry about that," the receptionist said as she opened the door for him. She eyed him from head to toe and back up to his face.

"Your clothes are over there. You may leave when you're finished dressing. Remember to take the papers with you and have your mother sign them. They must be returned to me within the next 72 hours."

As he dressed, Jason wondered again how much of what happened tonight had been staged. Was he supposed to feel frightened and trapped by a door that suddenly wouldn't open? Was that a warning from Zeus about what might happen if he ever crossed Zeus? Jason couldn't be sure of anything.

Chapter Nine

Youngsoo sat in the living room, listening while his sister argued with their father.

"I want to go back home. I was wrong about America being a better place than Korea. I want to go home today!"

"Absolutely not. You will never return to Korea. You left your shame there when you left. Now you are free to be a better person," her father told her.

"My son is not something shameful. He deserves a good life."

"Your grandmother will do her best to provide that for him. But you are forbidden to have any more contact with her or with your son. Do you understand? It is forbidden."

Youngsoo heard his sister stomp her feet as she went back to her bedroom, crying in anger.

He did not go to comfort her. He agreed with what his father was doing and that he had that authority over his daughter. Youngsoo held firmly to his belief that females are inferior and should only fulfill traditional roles, such as wife, mother, housekeeper.

In her room, Youngmi recorded a video of herself, which she posted as soon as she finished.

I am Youngmi Kwon. Some of you know me as a new student at Niagara County Public High School. I came from

Korea to America a few months ago, seeking a new life and a new start.

I thought that Americans would accept me for the person I am. But I was mistaken. The few people who I thought had become my friends have turned their backs on me. Why? Because my brother revealed my secret past to them. Now, everyone in school either ignores me or gives me hateful looks.

I did not share my past with anyone at school because my privacy is important to me. But there was also another reason. I feared the reaction that others would have, upon learning that I have a beautiful young son. I was forced by my family to leave him behind when I left Korea. Every day, my heart is broken, wishing that I could be with my little boy.

I want to return to Korea to raise my son properly, as a mother should. As I make this statement, I make a vow that I would rather die than live without my son, Ji-ho.

When you see me at school, would it hurt to say a kind word? Would it hurt you to understand my pain and have some sympathy for me?

I am begging someone, anyone, to help me. I want to escape from the hold my family has on me, so I can return to my true home and live my life as I wish to do.

Goodbye for now.

Comments to the video were varied. Many supported Youngmi. Others were not so kind. In fact, many of the commenters had vicious words for her.

Youngmi did not see any of the comments.

Hours later, her father called her for dinner.

No reply.

Her father grew angry, believing that his daughter was being insolent and disobedient. He went to her room and opened the door without knocking first.

"Ohhh no!" was all he could manage to say.

He never could have imagined the sight before him, though some might suggest that he should have predicted it.

Youngmi had thrown a rope over one of the beams in the ceiling of her room, with one end tied into a noose and the other end secured tightly to a locked window frame.

Tears streamed down her face as she climbed up on a chair, placed the noose around her neck, and kicked the chair away, strangling herself to death.

Mr. Kwon called Youngsoo into the room.

"Look what she did!"

Youngsoo showed no emotion. "What do you want me to do?"

"No one will ever know the truth. Purchase a ticket in her name for a flight to Korea. Everyone will think she went back. Do you understand the importance that this secret is kept between us?"

"Of course, I do, Father. As you wish."

Youngsoo understood the power of secrets. He knew that one day, this one might prove useful when the time came for him to assert himself as the head of ZEUS Universal Group.

"Mom, I have a surprise for you. Here," Jason said, handing her a large manila envelope.

"Oh, what's this? But wait, first tell me about the things I left for you. From your dad."

"He wrote such a beautiful letter. Do you want me to read it to you?"

"No, that's private between the two of you. But you were pleased with what he said, I take it."

"Very much. I never even knew he left a letter for me. I'm surprised you could keep it a secret all these years. Everyone knows you're an open book," Jason teased.

"Did you know about the family crest?" he continued.

"Oh yes. Beautiful, isn't it? I hope your father explained what the symbols mean. If not, do some research. You should appreciate your heritage more than you do, I think."

"Yes, Papa left it for me to pass it along to my son," Jason said, immediately regretting opening that door.

"I haven't heard you call him 'Papa' since you were a child," Katrina replied, ignoring the rest of Jason's statement.

"That's how he signed the letter. I didn't remember ever calling him 'Papa,' but now, that's how I'll always think of him."

"But Mom, open up your gift!"

"It isn't my birthday. Did I sleep through a few months and suddenly wake up to Christmas morning?" she asked, laughing.

She opened the gift from her son and gasped.

"How is this even possible? What is this, one of those Internet jokes where you prank your parents? Am I being secretly filmed?"

"No, Mom. It's real. You're all paid up. You don't owe the bank a nickel anymore."

As soon as Jason had awakened the morning after the photoshoot, he checked his bank balance. As a matter of fact, he checked it over and over, hardly able to believe it.

His balance had grown to a whopping $250,219.23, exactly $250,000 more than he had the day before. Zeus had come through for him, and suddenly, Jason Masters, or as he now preferred to be called, Ganymede, was rich!

He was waiting outside the bank when the branch opened, eager to be the first customer. He met the loan manager and paid the entire mortgage for his mother, both on the house and on the diner. He was provided with the deeds and other documents proving the debts had been paid in full, and he was proud to hand them over to his mom.

"I met with Zeus yesterday, after reading the letter from Papa, and it went very, very well. I'll fill you in on all the details, and I have some forms that you have to sign, but Zeus gave me an advance on the money I'll be making while I work for him. The first thing I did with the money was to make sure that you're debt-free."

"Oh, Cupcake, this is so sweet of you! What a wonderful young man you've become. But what do you mean, you'll be working for Zeus? What are you going to be doing? Working on an AI project?"

Jason told his mother some of what Zeus had told him about his position at the company, but was careful not to say too much, worried about the NDA. He didn't want to lose everything before he even got started.

"You're moving to Athens? That's down near Woodstock, isn't it?" she asked, mistaking Jason's destination as being Athens, New York.

"No, Mom, it's in Greece. But don't worry, I'll be safe and I can talk to you all the time, even every day. And I can send you money. I promise I'll take good care of you, like Papa wanted me to."

Katrina couldn't hide the tears in her eyes.

"Give me time to think about this," she told her son.

"I already took the advance money. I really need you to sign these papers for me. I have a deadline, and I lose everything if I'm late. Please, do it now. Do it so I can have a good future. I want to be the brightest star in the sky. Or, the brightest moon, since that seems to be my destiny."

"You promise to call me? Every day? Every single day, right, Cupcake?"

"I swear to you. I won't let you down."

Reluctantly, Katrina signed all the documents and handed them back to her son.

Just like the previous week, at 4:44 AM on Monday, Mr. Dawson, the principal, received another threatening message.

Last week was a test, my evil friend. Today, you will experience my wrath. All sinners at Niagara High will die by my hand. Your transgressions against me will never be forgotten nor forgiven.

"For the wrath of God is revealed from heaven against all ungodliness and unrighteousness of men, who by their unrighteousness suppress the truth." Romans 1:18

Shortly thereafter, a message went out to all members of the Niagara County School District community:

A threat has been received, once again targeting the Niagara County High School campus. We find no evidence that this threat is credible. All classes and activities at the elementary schools in the county will be held as scheduled. At the high school, there will be a two-hour delay for students.

All administrators, teachers, and other staff will report for work at their normal starting times.

The safety of our students is our highest priority.

Attendance at every school in the county was normal for a Monday. Teachers were given no instructions to discuss the threat with their students. The School Board had decided that the messages should be considered as hoaxes, but on the advice of counsel, they did notify the parents, in fear of being sued if anything ever did happen.

By the end of school on Monday, the threat had been completely forgotten.

At the high school, the hot topic of conversation among the students was the confrontation in the hallway between Timmy Connor and Youngsoo Kwon.

"Why did you spread that nasty, vicious rumor about Mimi? You know she did nothing wrong!" Timmy had shouted in rage when he first saw Youngsoo.

Youngsoo stood his ground.

"First of all, I did no such thing, as if it's any of your business," he sneered at Timmy.

"I stand up for my friends, especially my girlfriend!" Timmy answered, still shouting.

"Oh, now you have elevated your status to being the boyfriend? My sister did not speak of you as anyone special. Perhaps your feelings were on a one-way street?"

"Where is she? I want to talk to her!"

"Gone. She left yesterday, to return to Korea, just like she said she would in that horrible video, which of course was filled with lies and has been deleted. The person you describe as your girlfriend didn't even bother to leave a message for you. How embarrassing for you," Youngsoo continued.

"I can't even send her a text. My messages get rejected. I want to check in on her."

"You will never hear from her. She discarded her phone, just like she discarded you. She considered both you and her phone to be nothing more than American trash."

With that, Youngsoo walked away.

He was glad that his sister would no longer be a distraction for him. Even during the cremation, held in top-secret mode, he felt no remorse, no pain. A lifetime of believing that his fraternal twin should have been left to die as an infant shielded him from any sorrow that would be felt by any other twin.

"Meet me after school. Let's go have some fun. Word is you have money now. You feel like treating your boyfriend to something nice and very expensive?" Youngsoo teased, when he saw Jason at lunchtime.

"Not tonight. I have to work on my paper for English class tomorrow."

"Work on your paper? Why would you do that? You know that you're leaving this school, leaving the entire United States, in three weeks, right? Zeus is taking you to Athens when the line of products from the House of Ganymede is launched."

"I know, it might seem stupid. But as long as I'm a student here, I feel like I have an obligation to complete the assignments. Don't you feel the same way? Even though you'll be leaving for Athens shortly after I do."

Youngsoo, after thinking for a moment, replied, "Well, I'll turn in a paper. But only because Father does expect me to be an A-student. Otherwise, I'd just drop out."

"We can do something after school tomorrow. Not tonight. This paper, this particular assignment, has meaning for me. I want to do a really good job on it."

"However," Jason continued, "I do have to talk to you about something important. Something that happened with Zeus. It has me concerned. I'll tell you all about it later."

"The hell you will! You'll tell me right now," Youngsoo whispered, not wanting any other students to overhear their conversation. "Did Zeus do something to you? I'll kill him even sooner than I planned to if he did anything to hurt you."

Youngsoo took Jason by the arm and led him to an isolated area in the hallway.

"Spill it!" he demanded. "Tell me the whole story and don't leave out any details."

Jason pursed his lips and frowned.

"Maybe I'm being silly. I don't know ..."

"How can I protect you if I don't know what dangers you face?" Youngsoo said impatiently.

"Ok. There were no problems at the start of the meeting with Zeus. But he did tell me that I had to strip naked for an inspection. He said something like he had to see the merchandise before making an investment."

"Did he molest you? Did he?"

"No, nothing like that, though he made me feel like a piece of meat. I sort of expected he'd stamp me with 'Inspected by Number 10,' like you see on the beef at the supermarket."

"Is that all? You are being silly. Of course, he had every right to look at you. And I hope you're not telling me that you're ashamed to show off your body."

Jason sighed. "No, that's not all. The bad part came later. The part that has me worried that I might get blackmailed or something."

"You think you'll be blackmailed? How? What did you do? Did you betray me and get nasty with somebody?" Youngsoo demanded to know.

"This isn't about you, and no, I didn't betray you. I'm keeping myself pure for our first night together, just like you want me to."

With that, Youngsoo relaxed a little.

"So then, tell me. It can't be all that bad."

Jason described in detail what had happened during the photoshoot. Not the time spent with the designers, but the part where he had to perform as Supple, Rigid, and Beast. Jason blushed as he described his poses during the Beast portion.

"Do you think that sometime in the future, Zeus might use those photos to blackmail me, forcing me to do something I don't want to do?"

"No, I can assure you that will never happen."

"But you don't know how personal and intimate those photos are. They could destroy my reputation as Ganymede, I think, and I could lose the sponsorship."

"I just said that I can assure you that nothing like that will happen. Don't you want to know why I can make that assurance? These aren't just empty words. I always keep my promises."

Jason looked at Youngsoo, wondering what he meant.

Youngsoo looked away, then stared at the floor, slowly raising his head, saying, "Neither liquid nor wooden, during this phase I want to capture your animalistic nature. Begin with your aggressive masculinity. Act as men do when they are behaving badly. Then, transform to show your submissive, effeminate side. Do not be shy. Do not be afraid. Unleash the beast within. These photos will be the cream on top. Show me all of your hidden desires, your secrets, expose yourself for all the world to see!"

Jason was shocked, and it clearly showed.

"How do you know those words? Did someone show you? Did they tell you?"

Jason was shaking and close to crying.

"No, nothing like that. Don't you understand? It was me behind the mask. I was your photographer."

"Why? Why would you betray me like that?"

"Betray you? No, I wasn't betraying you. I was protecting you."

"That's what you call protection? Taking photos of me to blackmail me?"

"Hold on and let me explain. You have the wrong idea in your head. Father told me what Zeus was planning to do, to have naked photos taken of you. I begged Father to get Zeus to allow me to be there. That way, you wouldn't be exposing yourself to a complete stranger, and if necessary, since I have the original negatives, I can try to help if Zeus tries to use them against you."

"But Zeus has copies, right? He's seen them already?"

"Of course. Zeus is the owner and he sees and knows everything. But if he does try to blackmail you, I might be able to access his systems and delete everything."

"But why didn't you just tell me? Why all the secrecy?"

"I was sworn to secrecy. I had to sign an NDA and Father told me if I ever disclosed any of this information, I would be severely punished. So please, it's important that you tell no one. You already know how much people like to talk and if this ever gets out ..."

"Don't worry. My lips are sealed tighter than a dolphin's wetsuit."

Their laughter, as usual, diffused the tension, allowing the conversation to continue with no awkward feelings.

"One more thing," Youngsoo added. "I'm a little worried about Zeus blackmailing you, but I'm more worried he might try something else. I want you to promise me that if he ever tries to do anything to hurt you, or to touch you in a way that you don't like, tell me right away. I have a solution for that. Instead of waiting for the time I already plan to kill Zeus, I'll just do it sooner. I'll kill him on the spot to protect you."

"Don't worry, I can handle myself."

"No, not from him you can't. He's evil. You don't know him well enough yet. But you'll find out. In the meantime, get as much money as you can from him. Before you know it, we'll be strolling arm-in-arm on some Mediterranean beach together, and Zeus will be paying our way!"

"Europe will be our playground!" Jason agreed.

Jason spent Monday evening sitting at the desk in his room, working on his paper about *Tess of the D'Urbervilles*. Although it wasn't required for this assignment, he made sure to reference each element of a novel that Mr. Simmons had pointed out in class: plot, characters, setting, themes, point of view, and conflicts.

Jason wanted to impress his teacher. That was part of his nature, but he also had decided to confide in Mr. Simmons about his plans for the future, including leaving school, modeling for ZEUS Universal, and moving to Greece. He thought his teacher might have some good advice to offer.

When class began on Tuesday, the feeling in the room was somber. The desk and chair, where Youngmi would usually sit next to Timmy, had already been removed from the room. It was like the school wanted the students to forget she had ever existed.

And Mr. Simmons wasn't standing at the door to greet his students. Highly unusual.

As the students talked quietly, Mr. Dawson, the principal, entered the room, accompanied by an older man who looked somewhat haggard.

"Children, settle down. I have an announcement."

"We're not children. Mr. Simmons calls us 'ladies and gentlemen,' and you should respect us like that," Timmy called out.

"Children, be quiet. You should respect your principal more than to talk back like that," Mr. Dawson replied, in a tone best described as condescending.

Timmy folded his arms defiantly but remained silent, while the haggard-looking man slumped into the teacher's chair.

"This is Mr. Fuller, your new substitute teacher. You will listen to him the same as any other teacher in the school. Any disrespect will result in your immediate suspension. You have been warned."

Mr. Dawson hesitated before continuing.

"You will turn in your copies of the *Tess* novel. It's been decided that that particular book is too woke and you will not be reading it. The same goes for every title on the list that your former teacher gave you. Mr. Fuller will provide you with a new list soon. The School Board is still working on developing a list of approved books."

"Too woke? What the hell does that even mean? And where's Mr. Simmons?" Jason called out, defying the order from the principal to sit quietly.

Mr. Dawson stared at Jason, then at Timmy, and simply went out into the hallway, closing the classroom door behind him.

"Don't look at me," the new teacher said. "I don't know anything about it. I got a message early this morning, telling me to report to the school to start a new position today. They didn't tell me anything about what happened or why I'm here."

"I can tell you all you need to know," Debi said. "The School Board fired Mr. Simmons. They, including my mother, the President of the Board, decided that having a fag in the class-room is unacceptable. They also found out about all the woke literature that he was exposing us to, and they put a stop to that. And I'm glad they did. I don't want to be indoctrinated by their left-wing propaganda, and you should be thanking me that I'm protecting you from their influence, too. They're all a bunch of libtards."

Most of the class sat in stunned silence.

"You heard the young lady," Mr. Fuller said quietly. "We're here to do what the School Board tells us to do, so I want everyone to bring their books up here and leave them on my desk."

"Maybe you're here to do what the School Board says, but not me," muttered Jason, as he slammed his copy of *Tess of the D'Urbervilles* onto the teacher's desk.

"I'm going to protest at the next School Board meeting. The voices of the students should be heard!" Jason said to no one in particular.

"There won't be any protests, by you or anyone else," Debi retorted. "My mother canceled all the meetings for the rest of this year, because she refuses to be lectured by a bunch of woke libs who refuse to accept how the world really works, and who seem to forget who exactly is running the show."

"My father paid for these books. He doesn't need a meeting to contact the Board members to tell them what he thinks about this," Youngsoo said, as he returned his book, glaring at Debi as he walked by her.

"Are you even a citizen?" Debi retorted.

Youngsoo recognized this as the threat that she had intended, so he didn't reply. He wasn't sure how his father would want him to react. He showed no emotion, but on the inside, he was seething.

Jason tried to reach out to Mr. Simmons via email, but his school account had already been deactivated. Jason couldn't find him on any other social media. It seemed as though Mr. Simmons had completely disappeared.

How can that happen so quickly? Jason wondered.

First Youngmi. Then Mr. Simmons. Very peculiar.

That evening, Timmy sent a text to Jason.

"I'm so bored! I miss the fun we used to have before our disagreement. And my parents are gone for this whole week. You feel like coming over to play some videogames with me?"

Timmy sent a second text, hoping to convince his friend to accept his invitation.

"I already found the liquor my dad hid. I don't know why he even bothers. He knows I'm gonna find it and drink everything he has," accompanied by a googly-eyed smiley face emoji.

Jason stared at his phone. Our disagreement? It was so much more than that. But he recognized that Timmy was trying to make some amends for what he had said and done, so he waited just a few minutes before replying.

"Ok. But only if you promise to make me a vodka cran, extra strong, the way I like them."

Timmy was a bit surprised that Jason answered at all, but he was grateful for the opportunity to set things straight with his best friend since forever.

"Plenty of vodka, with just a hint of cran. The way we both like it. I'll be waiting on the porch."

Before their "disagreement," there had never been an awkward moment between Jason and Timmy. They were natural best buddies. Spontaneous laughter, jokes, just general fun, enjoying each other's company.

But not tonight.

Timmy was sitting on one rocker, while Jason took the other one, with a table holding their drinks between the two boys. Music was playing in the background, a playlist on Timmy's phone.

"This song is so awesome!" Timmy said, rising to his feet and dancing by himself to The Weeknd's "Save Your Tears."

Watching Timmy swaying in front of him, singing the words to this particular song directly to him, made Jason once again realize how much he loved Timmy.

He stayed silent through the entire song, just watching, feeling overcome with strong emotions. However, he also recognized the contradictions in what Timmy was doing, so he took a moment to consider his words.

"I'm confused. First, you send me a message about how you want to procreate and have like 10 babies. And now this? And after the way you treated me after our last time at the river? What's going on?"

Timmy walked back to his chair, sighed, reached for the bottle of vodka, and filled his glass to the brim.

"I'm sure you're confused. I'm confused, too. I don't even know who or what I am. All I do know for sure is that my life has been empty without you being a part of it."

He gulped down half the glass without a pause.

"I want to tell you a secret. It's a big one. Before I say anything, you have to promise to never tell a soul."

So many people with so many secrets, Jason thought. *How can high school life be this complicated?*

"You know you can trust me," Jason assured his friend.

Timmy finished his drink, while Jason hadn't even touched his.

Barely able to keep his balance, Timmy stood on the porch, facing away from his friend, not wanting to see his expression when Timmy told his secret.

"I'm a gay virgin," Timmy whispered into the night air.

"You're a what?" Jason asked, unsure he had heard him correctly.

Timmy turned and met Jason's eyes with his own.

"I'm a gay virgin. You heard me the first time. Why make me say it again?"

"Be more specific, Timmy. I want to be sure I understand. Are you a gay guy who's a virgin, or are you a straight guy that never had a gay experience, which would only make you a virgin concerning gay stuff?"

"Why can't you be serious about this? I'm trying to tell you something important about me. I'm gay. There, are you satisfied? And I'm a virgin. A total virgin, like I never did anything with anybody. But I want that to change. Right here. Right now. I want you to unvirgin me. And right after that, I want to unvirgin you."

Now it was Jason's turn to gulp down his drink. Seeing that, Timmy refilled his glass, thinking he had to get wasted if he was about to get unvirgined.

"First, is 'unvirgin' even a word?"

"If it isn't, it should be. That condition describes most people in the world, right?"

"But I have a more important question for you," Jason continued. "Suppose we do as you're suggesting. What happens after that? Will we be boyfriends?"

"Uhmmmm," came the reply. Timmy needed a minute to think.

"No, not boyfriends. Not openly. I don't think I could ever do that. I don't want to be the queer kid going to school dances and proms with another boy. I think it's too dangerous, especially in an area like this. You know very well that fags ... I mean, gays ... aren't really accepted here. Plus, my parents would kill me."

"And what do you expect, then? That you'll get married to a girl and have a couple kids, and just use me when you feel the need for a little man-to-man time on the side? You think I'm going to sit home alone knitting you sweaters and baking cookies, hoping you'll sneak in through my back door in the middle of the night, looking for a little back door action? What kind of life would that be for me?"

"You could marry a nice girl, too. Have a couple babies. Then we could sneak off and leave our wives taking care of the kids while we go play in the park or somewhere like that."

"What you're describing, Timmy, will never happen. Not for me. Not for us. Come here, I want to show you something."

Jason took Timmy's hand, which not long ago would have caused a thrill, but now he felt nothing but a gulf of emptiness between them.

"Look up there. Tell me what you see."

"The sky? What am I supposed to be seeing?"

Jason made a sweeping gesture with his free hand. "Look at the stars. There must be millions of them, right? And yet somehow, some of them capture our attention. The brightest ones."

"Yeah, so what?" Timmy asked.

"Think of those stars as people. Millions of people go unnoticed each and every day. But the bright ones — everyone sees them. They know their names. They're important, sometimes in ways that we don't even understand ourselves."

"Look at that one," Jason continued, pointing toward the north sky. "Look at its brilliance. And you know who that is? That's me. Because I shine bright. I stand out. People notice me and they're fascinated by me. I can't be bound to a small town in New York state where nobody does anything important. I was made for the world to see me and to love me. It's my destiny."

"You think you're that special? Really? Jase, you have really changed ever since you met that Asian boy."

Jason led Timmy back to the porch, and they both started drinking again. Then Jason told him about the job offer from

Zeus, how he'd soon be a supermodel spokesman for a line of men's beauty products.

"The launch is coming up soon. I'm going to be the face of IMMORTAL, from the House of Ganymede. That's my new name, Ganymede. Doesn't that sound sexy and glamorous?"

"You do know who Ganymede is and what happens to him, don't you?"

"What do you mean? Ganymede isn't a who, it's a what. It's one of the moons of Jupiter."

"You never were thorough with your research," Timmy chided him. "You always have to check multiple sources, and you can't rely on the first one or two that you see in a search engine."

"Well then, who is Ganymede? What did I miss?"

Timmy grabbed his phone and began to search, while Jason sat back in his chair, sipping his vodka cran, waiting for Timmy to tell him what he found.

"Well, yes, the first thing it tells me is about the moon of Jupiter, and then," Timmy said, as he scrolled through the listings, "then there's also a Ganymede in the stars."

"See, what did I just tell you? I'm a star and that proves it right there, on the Internet."

"Don't be silly. The fact that there's a star has nothing to do with you. But it's part of the constellation Aquarius, and sup-posedly, Zeus placed Ganymede up there, for some reason."

"So, it looks like Ganymede wasn't a person. It's a star or a moon. Case closed," Jason said, emptying his glass and reaching for the vodka bottle for a refill.

"Not so fast. Not so fast. Here's what I was looking for. Listen to this," Timmy said, and began reading from his phone.

"Ganymede was a beautiful shepherd boy, considered by Zeus, the King of the gods, to be the most beautiful of all the mortals. Giving in to his desires, Zeus took the form of an eagle, kidnapping the boy while he tended his flocks, bringing him to Mount Olympus, declaring the boy to be his cup-bearer."

Timmy looked up from his phone. "I guess a cup-bearer is like being a waiter. And you waited on Zeus at the diner. Ooooh, it's getting interesting now."

"Shut up and keep reading. Leave my personal business out of it."

"It says here that in some of the old poems, Zeus had a romantic relationship with Ganymede, though the storytellers differ in saying whether Ganymede was willing or not."

Looking up again, Timmy said, "I guess that might depend on the time when the poem was written. Whether it was acceptable to say that a god used a boy against his will. Like in the Puritan days, they might just skip over that part of the story."

"Why do you keep adding your own narration? What happens at the end? Does Ganymede live with Zeus and get a happily-ever-after or not?"

"Oh Jason, you won't believe this. Zeus grants immortality to Ganymede!"

"Wow, that's good! Isn't it?"

"Except that Zeus's wife, Hera, becomes jealous of Ganymede, since Zeus pays more attention to him than to her."

"Oh, a Greek soap opera!" Jason joked.

"Is Zeus married? The one you're gonna be working for? If so, you better keep an eye out for her, in case Zeus tries to get too cozy-cozy with you," Timmy said, winking and laughing.

He then continued, saying, "It gets even better. Hera harasses Ganymede endlessly, making his life unbearable. In one of the modern retellings, it's said that Hera poisons Ganymede."

"That can't be right. He's immortal. So what if gets poisoned?"

"Well, Ganymede can't die, but he can feel pain. And the pain inflicted on him by the poison is unbearable."

"So he lives a life of endless pain?"

"No, but I have bad news for you. In the end, Zeus can't bear to watch Ganymede suffer, so he does the only thing he can do. He takes away Ganymede's immortality, meaning that Zeus lets the poison kill him. But he did it because he loved the boy so much."

"Wow," Jason said. "To be immortal and then to die anyway. Those Greeks sure know how to make a story dramatic!"

"There's more. Zeus wants to immortalize Ganymede, so he sends his spirit to be among the stars, and that's why there's a star in Aquarius called Ganymede."

Timmy stopped his scrolling and returned to his drinking.

"I don't know. This story could be a warning. I wonder if that guy Zeus is out to kill you."

"Don't worry about that. I have a Protector."

"Who? Your new boyfriend?"

"None of your business," Jason said, not wanting to reveal too much.

They both sat silently for a few minutes.

"Dammit, Jason. I know you have a guy, but I have nobody. Now that Mimi went back to Korea, I'm all alone and I still wanna get unvirgined. Like, right now. Come on. Do it to me."

Timmy stood and started to fumble with opening his pants.

"Put it away and keep it away, virgin," Jason said, trying to make a joke out of what could be an awkward situation.

"I made a promise to someone to still be a virgin and save myself for a special night with him. He's going to bring me into manhood."

"I promise I won't tell anybody. Let's just do it. I know you want to. We can go inside if you're worried someone might see us."

"I already told you 'No.' I want to have a relationship where I can be honest with someone and not start off by having to lie to him, especially about something this important. I can't tell him I'm a virgin if I'm not."

"I can't believe we're even having this conversation. I can't believe you won't unvirgin me. But I'm not going to stay mad at you. Here. Drink up," Timmy said, lifting his glass and clinking it against Jason's.

"To gay virginity!"

Jason laughed. "Yes, to gay virginity! May it not last too long!"

They both laughed and drank, feeling the distance between them narrowing. It would never be the same as it was, but Jason never wanted to become enemies with his best friend.

"Dad, can I get a couple bucks? I need some more ammo."

"You're running low? Sure, Charlie. Doing a lot of target practice?"

"Yeah, I guess. Hey Dad, remember the girl in my English class I told you about? The one who was flirting with me?"

"Yeah, what about her?"

"I know she liked me. She even talked about the size of my dick right there in class. She wanted all the guys to know that she was interested in me," Charlie lied.

"That's how girls are. Possessive. Don't let her take control. I taught you better than that."

"She won't be taking control. She already left school and went back to Korea. They said she had a baby back there."

"Hmmm, nothing wrong with that. I knocked up your mother before we were out of high school, and we did all right. But since that baby wasn't yours, it's better you have nothing to do with her."

"I'll find one. There's plenty of girls in that school looking to get themselves a husband. I got my eye on a few prospects," Charlie said.

"Good. And keep up with that target practice, too. I've already told you that bad times are coming. I can feel it. One day soon, I'm gonna need your help to protect our property. You see how the immigrants are coming in every day and trying to steal everything from us."

"Don't worry, Dad. I'll be ready. Besides practicing at the range, I'm also spending a lot of time shooting at moving targets. Mostly squirrels and groundhogs. Getting pretty good at it, too."

"Good job, Son. Keep it up. We'll both be glad you did."

Chapter Ten

"I'm so bored!" Jason buried his face in his hands, frustrated at the slowness of the school day.

"Try to relax," Youngsoo told him. "Only 32 more minutes until another school week is over. Then you have another photoshoot over at ZEUS Universal today, right?"

"Yes, and this time maybe I won't be so nervous."

"Nervous? You didn't look nervous at all when I was taking those pix of you."

"I was nervous, but it also overwhelmed me. I'm not used to all that attention from the makeup artists, the hairdressers, everybody involved all focused on me."

"Get used to it. There's going to be so much attention on you. You're about to become world-famous!"

"Will my mystery photographer be there today, taking more nasty photos of me?"

"You call them 'nasty.' I call them erotic. And sexy. And HOT!" Youngsoo replied. "But no, I won't be there. Father wants me at home for a conference call with my sister, just to check up on how she's doing back home," he lied.

"Be sure to tell her I said 'Hi' and that I wish her well," Jason said.

"Ok, greetings from Jason. I'll tell her."

"Oh, let me tell you something before I tell anyone else. I'm not Jason anymore. I'm changing my name to Ganymede. That's going to be my professional name and my legal name. I won't even answer to the name 'Jason' anymore."

Youngsoo thought for a moment, recalling his earlier advice to Jason about never changing his name. However, he decided to place Jason's enthusiasm for his new role in life over his own misgivings, so he decided to be supportive.

"I think that's a good idea. Embrace your new personality. It suits you."

"I'm going to make an announcement video about it for my socials. My fans need to know, but like I said, I wanted you to be the first."

"Did you say you're supposed to get a second advance from Zeus after work tonight?"

"Yes, another quarter mil. I could get used to this real fast!" Ganymede said, grinning.

"You'll be a millionaire by the time we get to Athens!" Youngsoo said, clearly happy for his boyfriend.

As the final minute of class approached, Youngsoo said, "You know, we could just drop out and never come back here."

"True. But next weekend is the dance, and I want to make a big impression that night. The IMMORTAL product launch will be the day before the dance, and I want to show off for my friends here. I've known most of them for my entire life. And we won't be allowed into the dance unless we're still students."

Then, Ganymede lowered his voice, not wanting to be overheard. "After the dance, we'll drop out. To be honest, after that night, I'll be happy if I never see this place again."

Long after the last teacher had left school for the weekend, Mr. Dawson was still working in the Principal's Office. Before signing out of his district email, he remembered that he hadn't checked the spam folder all day. He knew from experience that he had to check, having missed some important messages in the past.

There it was — a threat that had been sent early Friday morning, but he had completely missed it.

Ignore my warnings at your own peril. My enemies, the unrighteous, will not inherit my kingdom. They will be vanquished and I will rule over my kingdom of glory in everlasting life. There will be bloodshed at Niagara High. The sinners will be punished. Final warning!

"Or do you not know that the unrighteous will not inherit the kingdom of God? Do not be deceived: neither the sexually immoral, nor idolaters, nor adulterers, nor men who practice homosexuality, nor thieves, nor the greedy, nor drunkards, nor revilers, nor swindlers will inherit the kingdom of God." 1 Corinthians 6:9-10

Why do I even bother telling anyone about these messages and waste people's time? It's clear they're hoaxes. Nothing happened here at school today, Mr. Dawson thought, as he deleted the message and went home for the weekend.

"I like your casual style today. You're looking so fine!" Ganymede told Youngsoo, who arrived at Jason's house in gray sweatpants and a graphic tee, showing Lady Gaga on her MAYHEM tour. "Where'd you get the shirt?"

"I flew down to Rio last night to see her. You were busy with the photoshoot at Zeus's, and my friend from Brazil called and invited me to the show. So, I went."

"Hold on. You're kidding, right? You flew to Rio last night just to see Gaga in concert? And you never said anything to me about it? As a matter of fact, you told me that you'd be on a family conference call with your father and sister."

"We did that," Youngsoo said, continuing to lie about Youngmi.

"And then I added something to my plans. You were busy. I already explained. You do understand that I know people, don't you? ZEUS Universal is a worldwide corporation, and I've been to many of their offices. I get to know people. The same will happen to you, sooner than you think."

"Who invited you? An old boyfriend? Someone you're seeing on the side?"

Ganymede immediately regretted making the comment.

"No, wait," he continued. "That's none of my business. It isn't like we're engaged — yet!"

Ganymede winked and laughed, though he felt somewhat left out.

"Did you have fun?"

"Trust me, you don't want to know how fabulous she was. What a show! It was a lot of fun, but I'll admit, I wish you'd been there with me. How'd the shoot go? Any problems I should know about?"

"It's like being in a different world, all these people paying attention to every detail about how I look. They already told me that Zeus loves everything we did for the next set of promos. And guess what was in my bank account this morning?"

"I already know," Youngsoo said with a knowing smile.

"All right, let's get busy with this. We want to find something to wear to the dance. I think we want to be noticed, but not overwhelm with our looks. What do you think?"

"I think we should just pick what we want to wear. No matter what, we're going to be noticed. Two guys dancing together. If we overwhelm them, well, I'd be okay with that," Ganymede answered.

"Speaking of dancing, do you even know how to dance?" Ganymede continued.

"Sure, I move my feet and arms a little and I wiggle my butt!" Youngsoo said, demonstrating his technique.

"No, that isn't what I mean. Did you ever do a slow dance with a guy? We don't wanna look like amateurs."

"You have a point. And the answer is no, I never did a slow dance with a guy. We should practice."

"Let's get some pointers online," Ganymede said, beginning to search for "two boys slow dancing."

They watched a few examples, with Youngsoo pointing out different options for how they could hold each other.

"We should find a special song and request it at the dance. That way, we can look totally cool during the first one," Ganymede suggested.

So, they searched for "slow dance songs," finding many results and listening to a few of the suggestions.

When they finally listened to "Endless Love," written by Lionel Richie and sung as a duet between him and Diana Ross, they knew they had the perfect song for them.

Youngsoo took Ganymede in his arms, and they began slowly moving to the tune. Then, with the sensuality of the music and the beautiful boy in his arms exciting him, Youngsoo took off his tee shirt, followed by Ganymede removing his athletic shirt.

"This is nice," Ganymede whispered, moving his hips against his boyfriend.

"Shhhh, just enjoy the feelings. No words needed," Young-soo said, reaching down to loosen his sweats, then stepping out of them, as if it were part of the dance moves.

Ganymede sighed deeply, seeing Youngsoo's taut, muscular body, clad only in red briefs, his body straining to be released from their hold.

"Take yours off," Youngsoo whispered to his dance partner, longing to see his beautiful body and to feel it against him.

Clad only in his white undies, Ganymede felt himself melting into his man. The song played on repeat, as their lips met and their tongues flicked and fluttered.

As they danced, Youngsoo took hold of Ganymede's hands, holding them high in the air, slowly increasing the pressure on Jason. Twisting, turning, struggling, their dance became a Daredevil Cartwheel, with one male eagle exerting dominance over another. Or, trying to. Neither eagle gave in easily, but when Youngsoo totally enveloped his partner in his arms, Ganymede was ready to surrender.

Panting with desire, he whispered, "Are we still going to wait, or ..."

Before Ganymede could finish the sentence, his bedroom door opened, his mother standing in shock, horrified at what she saw when she invaded her son's privacy, not bothering to knock.

"Oh, oh, I didn't know ..." she stammered, then slammed the door shut, never having imagined what her son had been doing.

Youngsoo looked at Ganymede, seeing his shocked expression, and though he wanted to be sympathetic, instead he burst out laughing.

"You know, she had to find out sooner or later."

"Yes, and I was planning on telling her. But for her to find out like this? It wasn't exactly what I had planned."

"You have to admit, it's kind of funny, isn't it? To be caught, well, not red-handed, but red-faced might be a better description."

Ganymede laughed. "You're right. She'll survive. She's no snowflake. Still, I better get dressed before I go talk to her," he said, laughing.

Katrina was in the kitchen, busying herself with making some hand-squeezed lemonade.

Hearing them enter the kitchen behind her, she turned and said, "You boys thirsty?"

She tried to put on a brave face, but then she sat at the kitchen table, buried her face in her hands, and began sobbing.

Ganymede walked over and sat across from her, taking her hands in his.

"Mom, I want you to meet Youngsoo. You already know about him, though I admit I didn't tell you everything."

Youngsoo walked over and shook Katrina's hand.

"Very nice to meet you, finally," he said. "I should be going so the two of you can talk. But I want you to know that your son is very important to me. That's all I'll say for now."

Ganymede got up and walked Youngsoo to the door, then returned to face his mother.

"Oh, Cupcake, I don't know what to say. I'm sorry I barged in on you, but I didn't know that you were ... busy."

"Mom, I've been wanting to have this talk with you for a long time."

"Just tell me. Say the words. I won't believe it till I hear you actually say it."

Ganymede looked away, then decided that this was no time to act indecisively. Looking his mother directly in the eye, he told her the truth.

"Mom, I'm gay. I hope you'll accept that. The guy you just met, I want you to know that he's my boyfriend. I want you to accept both of us."

Katrina looked at her son.

"I never suspected a thing. I always thought you were normal."

"I am normal. This is normal. That's something you have to understand."

"No, I don't understand. Not really. I need some time to think. I just don't know," she said, getting up from the table, going into her bedroom, and closing the door behind her.

Time slowed to a crawl as the two boys endured the torture of their final week at Niagara County High School. Sitting together during their final class, Ganymede said, "Will you pick me up tomorrow night and come inside so my mom can see us before we leave?"

"Of course, but only if you can guarantee that she won't attack me," Youngsoo joked.

"She still isn't happy, but at least she looks at me now when she speaks to me. For the first few days, she would talk to me by talking to Smiley and Polly. It was weird. She'd say things like, 'Girls, do you think Jason wants a cheeseburger for dinner?'"

"She still calls you Jason, then?"

"Yes. But she'll change. She just needs time to adapt."

Taking a look around at his classmates and his surroundings, Ganymede knew that this was the end for him. He wouldn't be back. The other students didn't realize it, but in his mind, he was already living the life of a rich, famous supermodel in Athens, using all of Europe as his playground.

The worldwide launch of the brand new line of men's beauty products, IMMORTAL by the House of Ganymede, was set for 5 PM on Friday.

Thirty minutes prior, a new video was posted to all of Ganymede's social media accounts.

I am Ganymede. You'll learn much more about me very soon. I'm excited and proud to be starting a new life. I appreciate all of my followers and I hope you'll join me on an exciting new journey. My love to all of you!

ZEUS Universal Group had employed an army of influencers to introduce the new campaign. Ganymede was trying to track everything, but it was impossible. First, thousands of views and likes. Then, hundreds of thousands, quickly climbing into the millions.

Orders for the products came pouring in, just as Zeus had anticipated. He knew the power of social media, as well as commercial messages on legacy media. He had chosen his spokesman well. Ganymede was an immediate hit as the face of the House of Ganymede.

Youngsoo sent a message, saying: "Congratulations! You are now the star that you deserve to be."

Ganymede was certain that he had made all the right decisions when he awoke the next morning to so many messages that it was impossible to reply to them all.

His thoughts for his future life were optimistic, and he was excited about the world of opportunities awaiting him.

Tonight, we're going to have so much fun at the dance. Everyone will already know I'm a superstar, and if there was any doubt that I'm now in a gay relationship, well ... there won't be any doubters after we dance together.

Plus, I'm finally going to get unvirgined right after the dance, he thought, remembering Timmy's wording for losing one's virginity.

Later in the day, Katrina knocked on her son's door, waiting for him to answer before she walked in.

"You see, I learned my lesson," she said to her son, who was seated at his desk, continuing to watch ever-increasing numbers of people liking and following his socials.

"How's that modeling thing going? Anyone interested?"

Ganymede showed his mother. Even she knew those numbers were impressive.

"I want to say something. I've never had any problem with gay people, but I always thought of them as someone else's children, not mine."

"But that doesn't even ..."

"I know it doesn't make sense. But understand that it's different when it becomes personal. I just didn't expect it to hit so close to home, and it shocked me. And now, I realize it makes no sense for me to accept other people's children as gay, but not my own."

"So, I want to make things right between us," she continued. "And I know you're going out to the dance tonight with your ... your boyfriend ... oh, I have to get used to saying those words."

Ganymede laughed, went over, and placed his arm around his mother, comforting her, feeling more comfortable in her presence than he had felt all week.

"I have a surprise for you," she told him. "I was pretending when I asked how your modeling was going. To be honest, it's all that everyone in town is talking about. I went out this morning and got some of the IMMORTAL products. They had some beautiful makeup for men. I didn't know that men would wear this, but I guess that's the idea, to get new audiences to try something new."

He hadn't noticed the bag his mother had brought into the room, filled with products from the House of Ganymede.

"What colors are you wearing tonight? We want the makeup to match the outfit, of course."

Ganymede laughed, knowing those were words that he never expected to hear his mother saying to him.

Youngsoo arrived, driving his own car. He had decided against using a limo, knowing that just the appearance of Ganymede, who had become an overnight star, would suffice to get the attention of all their classmates.

"Mom, I want to introduce you to Youngsoo, for the second time. Isn't it nice that we all have our clothes on this time?"

"Speaking of clothes, wow!" Youngsoo said. "You look like a movie star!"

Ganymede spun around, proud of his looks. Every piece screamed expensive and exquisitely tasteful, without a hint of being overdone. Black trousers with gold threading throughout were the perfect accent for his golden silk blouse. A single gold bracelet was worn on each wrist. He wore new diamond earrings in both ears, and of course, the thunderbolt necklace, a harbinger of good luck, danced at his neck.

"My mom did my eyes and my lips!" he proudly told Youngsoo.

"I did the entire face; give me the proper credit," Katrina joked, winking at Youngsoo.

"And look at you, what a handsome devil!" Katrina said to her son's date for the evening. "Let me take some photos, though I'm sure you'll take plenty at the dance tonight."

"My father is having the local press cover the event. Watch for us on TV later tonight," Youngsoo replied. "Having a local boy become an international star overnight doesn't happen every day, you know."

The scene at the dance was chaotic. Students and teachers were all trying to be seen with the newly-emergent star. Youngsoo was thrilled for Ganymede's success, without a hint of jealousy. He was confident enough in himself that he was happy to see others shine their brightest.

It took a while, but eventually, the dance got back to normal, which, like any high school dance, didn't lack for drama and excitement.

Youngsoo and Ganymede finally had a moment to sit and relax together at a table.

"Look over there, it's your old boyfriend, all by his lonesome. Maybe he wants to dance with you, too," Youngsoo said, pointing at Timmy.

"Can we get a pic with you two?" came a voice behind them. Turning, they saw two young teens standing hand-in-hand.

"We're freshmen, and we know you probably never even heard of us, but we know all about the two of you," the taller one said.

"We were inspired to come out tonight as a couple, just because of the two of you. We figured if you can do it, so can we."

Both Youngsoo and Ganymede stood to greet the boys, who introduced themselves as Angel and Nicky. After a few photos, they walked away, talking excitedly, as they immediately posted the new pix on their socials.

"Listen, it's our song," Ganymede said when "Endless Love" began to play.

They joined other couples out on the dance floor, but as far as they were concerned, they were all alone.

Neither of them noticed that Angel and Nicky were slow dancing right next to them, doing their best to emulate the two juniors they viewed as their teen idols.

Once more, Ganymede felt himself melding with his partner, as if their very beings were merging together, their hearts beating as one. They moved as if they were joined, without even thinking about it, effortlessly gliding along in sync with the music.

Ganymede was in the midst of a spiritual experience.

As the music faded into the next song, Youngsoo leaned in to whisper in Ganymede's ear, "I love you. I have always loved you. I will always love you."

"Somehow, I feel as though we're meant to be united. To spend a lifetime together. I love you, too," Ganymede replied.

And then, their first, public kiss, to seal the deal. No more hiding, no sneaking around, like Timmy would have wanted. Ganymede was declaring himself to be a proud, young, gay man, right there on the dance floor.

They could have danced like that forever, but Youngsoo decided to go over to where drinks were being served, to get some refreshments.

"Go wait for me at the table. Let me be the cup-bearer this time, before you leave for Olympus to serve Zeus."

Laughing, Ganymede did as he was told.

"Hey, this is the Crescent Moon Dance, not the Halloween Party," one of the chaperones said, seeing a student approaching the entrance, dressed in full camouflage and war paint.

The first shot caused confusion, as startled students weren't sure what caused the loud bang.

Then, screaming and running, as the chaperone dropped to the ground, killed instantly by the intruder.

"I come in vengeance! I come to destroy all of you! No one will escape my wrath and my fury! You are the witnesses to my power and my glory!"

The shooter took to one knee and began firing indiscriminately into the crowd. Though the carnage lasted for less than 30 seconds, witnesses would later describe the experience as lasting for 2 or 3 minutes. The horror of the moment would cloud anyone's judgment.

Youngsoo dropped his drinks as soon as he realized what was happening, running to shield his Ganymede from harm.

What he witnessed will haunt him forever. Ganymede's lifeless body lying on the ground, in a pool of blood, his face splattered red, his spirit gone.

"Noooooooooooo!" The guttural scream from Youngsoo was the only sound he could hear, unaware of all the other anguished cries around him. Turning, Youngsoo watched as the shooter turned the gun on himself, blasting himself into oblivion.

Youngsoo laid himself over Ganymede, desperately trying to will him back to life.

All he could hear was his own beating heart, so loud that he became deaf to the screams and anguished cries around him. Ganymede's heart, once in sync with Youngsoo's, lay silent, unmoving, still. No matter how hard he embraced him, Youngsoo could not find a way to bring Ganymede back.

I need the power of the gods, he thought. *I need the power to grant immortality, like in the Greek story of Ganymede. If I had the power of Zeus, my Ganymede would live forever, to rule as a king, just as he was destined to do in this lifetime.*

Youngsoo felt strong arms lifting him up, trying to carry him away. But he struggled to remain with his love. The thought of having to go through life without his chosen one was unbearable.

"We're outside the scene of tonight's horrific shooting at Niagara County High School," the newscaster said, talking into the camera.

"A scene of chaos and despair. We're told that there are multiple casualties, some fatal. We're waiting for a statement from the police chief. Oh, he's coming out right now."

The chief walked solemnly to a spot in front of multiple news cameras.

"I have grim news to report. Our community has suffered a shock, with an attack at this school, the heart of the community. First, let me assure all members of the community that there is no imminent danger to anyone else. The perpetrator of this horrific crime killed himself before any first responders could arrive."

He ignored questions being shouted at him by the reporters.

"Immediate family members of the deceased have been notified. Therefore, I can now publicly release their names. These young people had their lives stolen from them. It's with profound regret that I will now say their names."

"First, Mr. William Casey, who worked as a teacher's aide and was present tonight as a chaperone.

Second, Tevin Jackson, a junior, a star student and a star athlete on the football team.

Third, Susan Malone, also a junior, and a member of the National Honor Society.

Fourth, Paul Turner, a senior, and a member of the student government.

Fifth, Jason Masters, a junior, who was here celebrating the start of his new career as a spokesman for ZEUS Universal.

Finally, the shooter, identified as Charles Bannon, also a junior. More details will be provided about him at a later time. We ask that everyone keep the families of the victims in your thoughts and prayers. We'll give regular updates as we receive more information."

"Oh, I almost forgot," he continued. "Injured victims are being treated at multiple hospitals in the area. There are over a dozen with injuries, some life-threatening. Family members can get specific information by contacting us."

With that, the chief walked away, conferring with his deputies about next steps.

Of course, family members had rushed to the area when the news first broke. Mr. Kwon, like many others, searched desperately until he found his son, who was huddled on the steps outside the building. His clothes were covered in blood, making Mr. Kwon think his son had been injured, screaming for a medic to help Youngsoo.

After determining that he had not been injured physically, Mr. Kwon immediately became concerned for his son's emotional health.

"The best thing for us to do is to get far away from this evil place. We're leaving for Athens tomorrow. I never want to see this place again."

"No, Father. I know you're trying to help, but I won't leave tomorrow. You can go, and I'll follow in a few days. I have to be here for ... for ..."

He couldn't say the words, but his father understood that Youngsoo wanted to stay to attend the funeral services for Ganymede.

Katrina almost crashed her car as she drove back home from the scene, blinded by tears, shaking uncontrollably. She was haunted by the scene at her home. Ganymede's two Frenchies, Smiley Myrus and Polly Darton, were sitting expectantly on the front porch, waiting eagerly for the return of their best friend. Katrina urged them to come inside, but they refused.

The next morning, they continued their vigil. Every day, at the time Ganymede would normally get home from school, they'd wait on the porch, lying against each other for comfort, upset that there was no sign of the one they loved the most.

A sense of shock enveloped the entire community.

This has always been a safe area. How could this happen here?

Everyone involved, especially friends and family members, constantly asked themselves the one question that can never be answered: Why?

Katrina became despondent, withdrawing into her own world, wondering how she would survive without her only son.

Youngsoo was inconsolable, moving from feelings of extreme anger to unbearable sadness.

Everyone sensed the eerie silence left behind by the victims, who had once filled the lives of those they knew with joy and laughter. Not that they were perfect, but people always tend to remember the good times rather than the bad.

Zeus, faced with making an important business decision, went ahead with the promotions, still using Ganymede as the face of IMMORTAL. He wanted to see the reactions of his customers, and he wasn't disappointed by them.

Of course, word of the death of Ganymede spread quickly through the social media universe, with many people, including celebrities, expressing their shock and their condolences. Zeus had his influencers double down, posting that it was in tribute to Ganymede that his promos would continue to be used to honor him. Customers agreed, not only with comments, but with purchases. Sales were stronger than even the best estimates, with huge profits coming in for ZEUS Universal Group.

According to the contract signed by Ganymede, his mother was the sole heir to his earnings, so Zeus ordered that the commissions earned on all of the IMMORTAL products would be paid directly to Katrina.

"Look, Father, have you ever seen anything like that?"

Youngsoo, his father, and Zeus were at the Niagara Falls International Airport, seeing Mr. Kwon off as he headed to Athens. Zeus and Youngsoo planned to leave Niagara in a few more days.

"What is that?" Mr. Kwon asked, looking up at the sky.

Several pairs of eagles had taken flight at the same time, circling the area as if they were on a mission.

"Twelve. I see twelve of them," Zeus said. "There's only one explanation. Those are the 12 gods of Olympus, circling, searching for Ganymede. But he's been lost, and they will just continue searching in vain. This is a tribute from the gods. That's the only possible explanation."

The day of Ganymede's funeral found Youngsoo filled with dread. He didn't like the rituals associated with Western funerals. Like many in Korea, he found cremation to be preferable to burials, but he had no say in the matter here.

There was no church service. Katrina had no strong re-
ligious convictions, and neither did her son. She decided it
would not have honored his memory to pretend otherwise.

In a private moment, with the casket open, Katrina gazed
at her only child, despondent. She walked up to him, touched
his hands, and placed two objects into the casket.

Feeling the coldness of his hands horrified her, as she gently folded the letter from his father into them and placed the
family crest on his chest.

She noted that, at her request, the gold chain with the
lightning bolt pendant, which had been gifted from Youngsoo,
was around his neck.

Her final action was to brush two fingers against her own
lips, then pressing them against Jason's lips. A final kiss goodbye.

She backed away, terrified at the thought that she would
never see her Cupcake again.

Her only other request was that the service should end
before the casket would be lowered into the grave. She knew
that she couldn't bear to witness that, and she didn't want to
inflict that pain onto others.

There was a large crowd assembled for the final rites. Katrina was seated on a folding chair, staring at the coffin holding
the body of her son, wondering what she would do without
him. Ever since the night of the attack, she alternated between
uncontrollable sobs and moments of such extreme darkness
that she felt lost, disoriented, abandoned.

She did not speak at all, other than to whisper a few words
to those who came forward to offer words of condolence.

Several of those in attendance did speak, including Timmy.

"I wrote this poem for one of my class assignments, but I
was thinking of Jason at the time I wrote it. When I shared it
with him, I'll be honest and tell you that he didn't really like

it, but he misunderstood my intentions. I was trying to honor him," he said, as he tried to choke back his tears.

"I want to dedicate this poem once again to my best friend. I changed a few of the words, because of what happened, and also because of what he told me."

Tears of anger and pain clouded his eyes, but he didn't need to see the paper he was holding. He knew the words and could recite them without notes.

Eggs crack, bros chirp
Into a world of hunger and cold
The warmth of Mama
Shields him from the biting winds
Jason is Eagle

Father strong
In regal flight
I watch to learn
I must survive
Jason is Eagle

Solo flights
Days and nights
In search of prey and
For his mate, not to procreate,
But to love, in spite of hate
Jason is Eagle

The arrow strikes
His spirit flies
Limp body falls
Failure is mine
Jason is Eagle

He should have soared
And ruled the skies
Life wasn't fair
All alone he died
Ganymede was Eagle

When he finished, Timmy walked over to Katrina, hugged her for as long as he could, then tore himself away, leaving the site. He couldn't stay to watch the rest of the service.

Youngsoo did not join the group at the graveside service, though he watched from a distance. He did not want to share his grief with others. For him, this was very private. Just between him and his Ganymede.

He waited until everyone had left, planning to spend time alone with his soulmate, but the workers from the cemetery began their approach, ready to remove the timber baulks from under the coffin, to begin the process of lowering it into the ground.

Youngsoo stood close by, watching in horror as the coffin disappeared from view. Then, he decided that he had to act.

"Wait! Stop what you're doing!" he shouted, as the men began using the bulldozer that would cover the coffin forever.

"Who are you? What are you doing here?" the foreman asked him.

Youngsoo gave a very brief explanation and handed out bribes, asking only that the workers leave the grave uncovered until the next day. They reluctantly agreed to leave the work undone for a few hours, but insisted that they had to finish the work before the end of their workday, which would give Youngsoo a few hours.

They left the area, leaving Youngsoo alone.

He sat, cross-legged, at the edge of the grave, looking down at the expensive coffin wherein lay the earthly remains of the one Zeus had called the "most beautiful mortal."

Expecting to feel at peace, Youngsoo closed his eyes, calling for the spirits of his ancestors to join him, perhaps to accompany the spirit of Ganymede during the next part of his journey.

"You think I only knew you for a short time," Youngsoo said aloud, "but I've known you for a very, very long time. I remember you so well. We meet in every lifetime, having adventures. We conquer worlds. And yes, we love each other every time we meet, throughout many centuries of human history."

He paused, gathering his thoughts.

"This time, I thought we would conquer Zeus together. It was almost too perfect. We had all the tools we needed to accomplish our goals. But then, this horrible thing happened, and you were snatched away from me."

Another, longer pause.

"I'm not angry. Not at you, of course. Because I know that we'll meet again in the future. But because your stay this time was so short, I hope that you'll wait to return so that we can be reunited and once again be the same age. If you return too soon, I might be too old for you, or we might miss each other altogether."

Youngsoo continued, speaking as though Ganymede was sitting there right in front of him.

"I foresaw your destiny, and it was strong. But we made one error. Do you remember when I warned you about changing your name? When you went ahead and changed it anyway, your destiny was changed. And I stupidly went along with it. But I did that because I saw your excitement when you were about to become a star.

But in the old Greek stories, Ganymede was never a hero. He was a victim. His story is a tragedy. I should have remembered that, and I should have forbidden you from changing your name. And now, it's too late. Your story also turned into a tragedy, and I played a part in making it that way."

Grief causes people to react in irrational ways. As Youngsoo stood, never taking his eyes from the casket, his calm demeanor turned into an uncontrollable rage. A flash flood of raw emotion broke through the dam that had been restraining his emotions. Though he had just said that he wasn't angry, his flashing eyes and menacing look said something else.

"I wanted you to be my partner in conquering Zeus, but you left me too soon," he shouted.

"How can I accomplish this without you at my side? This is all my fault, because I walked away and wasn't there to protect you when you needed me. But you let me walk away. You could have been next to me the entire time!"

Tears began streaming down his face.

Needing a way to vent his sudden turn toward anger, Youngsoo saw that there were rocks in the dirt that would soon cover Ganymede's casket. He picked one up and dropped it into the grave, where it landed with a thud atop the box.

"Damn all the gods!" he shouted, picking up another rock and hurling it into the grave with all his might.

"Damn you! Damn you! Damn you!" he shouted, over and over, throwing more rocks at Ganymede's final enclosure, tossing his head back so he faced the sky, screaming an inhuman sound of eternal grief and everlasting sorrow.

Barely able to breathe, Youngsoo forced his feet to move him away from the site. He was unaware that Timmy, who had spent the afternoon trying to drown his sorrows with a bottle of vodka, had fallen asleep behind one of the gravestones, out of sight. Timmy had awakened in time to hear everything that Youngsoo had said, but he had no idea how to react or respond. He curled up on the ground and fell asleep once more.

Waking a few hours later, Timmy was startled to find himself in the cemetery, in the dead of night. He was even more shocked to find Youngsoo sitting at his side.

"I found you here when I was in despair about everything that happened," Youngsoo said, "and I decided that you should not wake up alone and afraid. It's better to be with someone in times of great sorrow."

Timmy sat upright, trying to orient himself, pulling himself from the ground, grasping at Youngsoo's hand. Though he still held Youngsoo responsible for the disappearance of his sister, Timmy was grateful for the company.

"Look up there," Youngsoo whispered. "Look at all the stars. And you know that the brightest of them all is right there," he said, pointing at one star outshining all the others.

"That, my friend, is our Ganymede. He will always be there, looking over us, guiding us, in whatever we do. We're going to be okay, as long as we follow his guiding light."

What does it mean to be immortal?

Some say that as long as a living person remembers you, then you are kept alive in that memory.

Some believe that no person can ever be truly immortal, while others would argue that some people are never forgotten, such as historical figures known by many, even centuries after their mortal lives ended.

Can "things" be immortal? Can a star last forever? Even if it does, if it has no life, how can it live forever? Is the mere existence of an object enough?

Or maybe immortality can be found in the symbolic world. Ancient Egyptians considered the ankh to be the symbol of immortality, believing that their gods lived forever.

Ancient Greeks and Romans told the stories of their immortal gods, and those stories still live on today. Maybe they have achieved immortality.

Talk with anyone who knows their cultural history, and you're sure to find at least one story of this nature.

The Christian bible describes its god as immortal. "Now to the King eternal, immortal, invisible, the only God, be honor and glory forever and ever. Amen." (1 Tim. 1:17)

Millions believe in the immortality of the human soul. Religions describe their versions of the afterlife as being authentic, requiring faith, since no proof can ever be shown.

Many also believe that there's a type of immortality when a person passes on their DNA to their descendants. But how long does that last? In America, with its youth-based culture, how many people know anything about their great-grandparents?

Youngsoo thought about all of this as he pondered his future in this life without Ganymede. His belief in reincarnation was unshaken. He has memories of past lives. He believes this as a core truth, and it's as apparent to him as his earthly memories of every day of this life.

He knows that his soul will once more meet the soul of Ganymede. Without that belief, his life would be without meaning. In this lifetime, he's still determined to conquer Zeus and to take control of his empire. Even if he can't share it with Ganymede, he'll stop at nothing to take control.

Three months later, Katrina continued to go through the motions of living, though she felt as if she had died the same day as the school massacre.

Despite having money for the first time in her life, she only had one desire. To see her son again. To hear his voice. To see him playing with his dogs before heading out to school. To have him working with her at the diner. Just one more time to sit together out on the porch, enjoying the sunset, and chatting as mother and son.

She could buy anything she wanted. Except that.

"I'm clocking out now," Maria said. "Can I buy you a coffee? You look like you could use a friend."

"Sure, let's get a table," Katrina said to her employee, who had been working at the diner for almost as long as Katrina had owned it. "But don't clock out. Let's do this on company time," Katrina said, in her first attempt at humor in months.

Maria poured the coffees, then sat across from Katrina.

"I hope you won't mind if I speak plainly. I'm not good at fancy talk."

"Please, say what's your mind," Katrina said.

"I see you here every day, working, trying to be normal, but I sense that your soul has left you. You seem to be ... empty. But I'm not trying to insult you. Please don't take it that way."

"I'm not insulted at all. What you're saying is the truth," Katrina assured her.

"I'd like to offer some advice. Take it or leave it, as you decide. But I think you had a purpose in life, which was to care for your son, and now, maybe, you're not sure if you have a purpose anymore."

Katrina hung her head, feeling a sense of shame.

"I don't know what to do."

"No one can decide for you," Maria told her. "But I had an experience which, while different from yours, affected me in the same way."

"What happened?"

"You know that I have a child who went through a transformation ... a transition ... from one stage of life to another. I lost someone, but I also gained someone new. But it wasn't an easy process. Not for her. Not for me. And then, when she was attacked ..."

"Yes, I remember when you took time off to help her recover."

"And I appreciated so much how you gave me all the time I needed. But my Margarita isn't the only one. It happens to so many of them. And they need help. They need resources. They need support that in most cases, their families can't or won't provide."

"What are you saying?" Katrina asked.

"I'm saying, instead of spending a lifetime in solitary sorrow, think about what your son would have wanted you to do. Can you imagine, if he's looking down on you, that he'd be happy to see you wasting the rest of your life? All I would ask is that you give that some thought. How can you honor his memory?"

Katrina sat upright, feeling alert for the first time in months.

"Oh Maria, you're so right. What have I been doing? Thank you for having this talk with me!"

Maria had given Katrina an idea, but she needed guidance. She began researching foundations and how they work to benefit their communities. But she needed more, so she started to contact people directly involved in that line of work.

She sent a message to Youngsoo, who replied:

Katrina,

Thank you for contacting me. What a wonderful idea you have! I can assure you that ZEUS Universal Group will not enforce any trademark rights against you. Please proceed with our blessings. And, in support of your efforts, please accept a personal contribution from me in the amount of $1 million. I wish you great success!

Youngsoo

Six months later, Katrina found herself in front of a crowd of people, who had gathered at the new LGBTQ+ Resource Center, located on the main street of Niagara, New York.

Greeting those present, she said, "Thank you to everyone who came out to celebrate our grand opening today. This project has been completed in memory of a very special person. My son was named Jason by his father, who saw his blonde hair and thought of Jason and the Golden Fleece.

Jason was a victim of gun violence, but I don't want him to be remembered as a victim. My son was also a member of the LGBTQ+ community. Specifically, he was gay, and he was proud to be gay. When he told me, well, I'll be honest, it took me a minute to accept it. But what kind of parent would I be if I had rejected him over something that was within his nature?

Around the same time he came out to me, Jason was also chosen to be the face of IMMORTAL. You know, the beauty products. It was in that spirit that Jason chose to change his name to Ganymede.

I accepted and loved my son as a gay teenager named Ganymede. But it was rare for me to call him anything but my special name for him. He was my Cupcake."

At that signal, a line of waitstaff emerged from the restaurant area of the center, mingling among the guests, holding trays of cupcakes decorated with rainbow frosting, serving them with pride.

"Please welcome some of our new employees, who've been very busy baking some special cupcakes for you to enjoy, in honor of my son," Katrina continued.

"When he was killed, I was deeply depressed until a very wise woman counseled me to find a way to honor my son's memory. So, today we celebrate the grand opening of this center. We have counseling services available, focusing on LGBTQ+ youth. We also have a library, a restaurant, a technology center, and upstairs, we have rooms for people to find shelter, especially when hate drives them out of spaces that were once safe, but might have become dangerous."

Fighting back tears and looking upward as if trying to see her son once more, she said, "I'm so proud of all the people who helped bring this project to life."

Stepping to the side, she watched, along with the audience, as a curtain opened to reveal the wide banner behind her, proudly proclaiming:

Welcome to the House of Ganymede!

The End

Also by

Robert A. Karl

- DRAG WARS: Fangula vs Pridezilla

- The Goldies: 50th High School Reunion

- <u>The CLUBBED Trilogy</u>

- CLUBBED: A Story of Gay Love: Trials, Tribulations and Triumphs

- CLUBBED TWO: Anxiety, Anger, Activism

- CLUBBED THREE: Darkness and Light

The author welcomes ratings and reviews submitted by readers, especially when posted to Amazon and Goodreads.

About the author

Robert A. Karl is an award-winning Queer author. Originally from Philadelphia, he now lives in San Juan, Puerto Rico.

Visit the author's website at: robertkarlauthor.com

Visit the author's online shop at: clubpride.org

Contact the author at: robert.karl.author@gmail.com

www.ingramcontent.com/pod-product-compliance
Lightning Source LLC
Chambersburg PA
CBHW071603180626
46819CB00002B/109